SUB ROSA

MARVEL
CAPTAIN AMERICA™

SUB ROSA

David McDonald

JOE BOOKS LTD

Published simultaneously in the United States and Canada
by Joe Books Ltd, 567 Queen St. West, Toronto, ON M5V 2B6

www.joebooks.com

Library and Archives Canada Cataloguing in Publication
information is available upon request.

ISBN 978-1-772752-01-4 (print)
ISBN 978-1-772752-03-8 (ebook)

First Joe Books Edition: June 2016
3 5 7 9 10 8 6 4 2 1

Printed and bound in Canada

To my Muse. You know who you are.

To Joe Simon and Jack Kirby—thank you for creating
a timeless hero who will never go out of fashion,
and whose virtues will never be obsolete.

Chapter 1

Steve Rogers dove behind a fallen tree as bullets, humming past his ears like angry wasps, sliced leaves off the branches around him. Even in the middle of the evasive maneuver, his mind identified the distinctive sound of AK-47s set to full automatic fire. It was no wonder his subconscious was familiar with it; he had come across the ubiquitous weapons—or their counterfeits—on a hundred battlefields since he had woken up in this brave new world. Familiarity hadn't bred contempt, though, and he had a soldier's healthy respect for the weapon's utility, especially in capable hands. And the men shooting at him were far too capable for his taste.

Rogers took a deep breath, then launched himself from behind the log. His muscles flexed beneath his tricolored uniform, working in perfect harmony as he sprinted across the clearing in a blur of red, white, and blue. With a single fluid motion, he reached over his shoulder for the shield strapped to his back and sent it spinning through the air. The concentric red circles on white, inset with a white star on a blue field, echoed the patriotic shades of his uniform, but were now merely blurs as the shield whistled through the air. A series of wooden thumps sounded as the shield ricocheted from trunk to trunk, followed by meatier sounds as it struck flesh and bone. Rogers stretched out a hand just in time to catch the shield; it thrummed slightly in his grip.

Steve had counted the sounds of bodies hitting the ground, and, knowing that one man was still standing, brought the shield up in front of his face just in time to block a hail of bullets from the gun fired by the last of his assailants. The shooter squeezed the trigger in panic rather than letting off short, controlled bursts, and the gun pulled up, giving Rogers the opportunity he had been waiting for. Before the other man could react, Steve crossed the space between them, diving under the arc of fire. His shoulder hit the other man's midriff in the sort of tackle Rogers had dreamed about laying on someone back when he had watched the jocks playing football—from the sidelines, of course.

Rogers was almost a hundred pounds heavier than he'd been then, and it was all muscle—the other man didn't stand a chance and his breath left his body with an anguished grunt as he was driven to the ground. Rogers knelt over him and delivered a precise blow to his temple that rendered him unconscious.

Steve glanced around to be sure that was the last of his assailants, and then sprinted into the trees, heading in the direction of the site he had been shown on the map back at HQ. He was moving on instinct now, veering seemingly at random around anything that appeared out of place. It might have been nothing, but his finely honed combat skills told him that a slight difference in color or texture might hide a land mine or a trip wire.

Rogers froze, then darted behind a tree just before three more men came running along the faint outline of a path. They could have been stamped from the same mold—short and stocky with hard, cold eyes and AK-47s held across their chests. As they passed his hiding place, Steve stepped out behind them. One was down before he knew anyone was there, knocked out with a blow from Rogers' shield. Steve's fist crunched into the chin of the second man as he turned around, sending him sprawling. Steve ducked a razor-sharp machete that cut though the air where his head had been; rigid fingers stabbed into its wielder's solar plexus, followed by a knee coming up to meet the man's descending face.

The whole fight lasted only a matter of seconds, and Rogers wasn't even breathing quickly. He resumed his run through the woods, keeping parallel to the trail and using the natural cover to mask his approach. He was almost on top of his objective now, and stopped to assess his options. From the edge of the trees, he could see that the site was nothing fancy—a large canvas tent with no walls, its floor space taken up by long tables. A number of women and young men in surgical masks were lined up along the sides of the tables, some weighing out piles of white powder, others bundling it into compact bricks. A number of guards strode back and forth, occasionally stopping to examine the work going on under their watchful gaze.

Steve, concealed behind the branches with sunlight shining through leaves and dappling his face with tiger stripes of shadow, watched for almost half an hour. Slowly, a subtle pattern emerged in the guards' movements, one that they might have been unaware of, but that was evident to Steve's trained eye. As soon as the moment presented itself, Steve was up and running, his shield flying through the air and taking out the first of the guards. Before the others could bring their weapons to bear, Steve was on them. Realizing quarters were too close for guns, the guards drew other weapons.

Five of the six men were armed with machetes; the sixth man held a gleaming straight razor. His grin was almost as dangerous looking as the razor was—right up until Steve's boot landed squarely in the middle of his face. As the first guard went flying, the man nearest to Steve slashed out with his machete, but Rogers grabbed his assailant's wrist, holding it in an iron grip while his other fist crashed into the attacker next to his foe. The man went down and Steve pivoted, throwing his captive over his shoulder and into the man coming up behind them. Neither guard got up, leaving

Steve free to deal with the rest. They were good, but Steve was better. In a matter of seconds, he was the only man left standing.

Rogers turned and looked at the stunned workers, who were frozen with fear. Some were on their knees, hands clasped in prayerlike gestures, while a number were huddled together, sobbing. Steve felt a flash of guilt—he knew that the workers were little more than slaves, pawns in a game they could not understand.

"You're free," he said gently. "You can go."

The only response was uncomprehending stares, and he realized that the people couldn't understand him. He tried the few words of Spanish he'd picked up over the years, but there was not even the slightest hint he was getting through to the workers. He sighed, reached down to free the strap of an AK-47 from around the back of an unconscious guard, and pointed the gun into the air. He pulled the trigger, letting off a short burst of gunfire and stitching a line of holes in the canvas of the tent's roof. Some of the workers screamed at the sound, while others were beyond even that, such was the extremity of their fear.

"Please, get out of here," Steve yelled. "I'm not going to hurt you, but you need to go. Now."

The workers might not have understood Steve's words, but the gunshots spoke a universal language. Without a backward glance they rushed into the jungle, leaving Steve alone among the tables. He ran a finger along one, his lip curling in disgust at the film of white powder on his gauntlet. He pulled the utility belt from around his waist and took out a number of small, oblong objects. Systematically, he placed the devices around the tent. After they were all positioned, Rogers dragged the unconscious guards one by one into the jungle, tying them to trees no closer than thirty yards away from the tent. As Rogers grabbed the last guard, he hesitated for a moment, then seized a couple of the white bricks and stuffed them into the man's shirt.

Steve checked the knots on the ropes, making sure that they were firm enough to hold the men even if they woke, and then pulled out a small sphere with a flashing blue light that he placed on the ground between one of the men's boots. A team made up of a mix of agents from the local government and the CIA would come to arrest and question the men, and the beacon would guide the authorities straight to the prisoners. Technically, his role in this joint exercise was now finished and it was time to leave, but Steve had one more thing to take care of. He'd left enough of the drugs to make the charges stick, and for a team of chemists to analyze the narcotics and provide the data required to track the spread of this particular cartel's influence, but Rogers—like his superiors at S.H.I.E.L.D.—was enough of realist to know that if there was too much temptation, some of the drugs would conveniently disappear. As he turned back to the jungle, Steve pulled a black, rectangular box the size of a small book from his pocket. Extending an antenna, he raised a hinged flap on the front of the box, revealing a red button. Without hesitation, he pressed down on it, hard.

The jungle air was split by a cascading series of explosions, and smoke and flames billowed high into the sky. Rogers didn't flinch, even when a smoking fragment of table crashed a few feet to his left. Behind him, what was left of the site burned briskly, thousands of dollars a second going up in smoke. Steve reached up to the side of his head and touched the transceiver that nestled snugly in his ear.

"It's done," he said softly.

"Roger that, Captain America." Steve winced at the loud crackle in his ear. "Proceed to the rendezvous point and prepare for extraction."

"Roger." Steve grinned. "Get to da choppa."

"Ah, we have some interference; please repeat."

"Never mind," Rogers said. He didn't want to explain that his catch-up movie and TV viewing since his return had only made it to the mid-1980s. "On schedule to meet the chopper."

"GPS tracking has you at four miles out. You're going to have to hustle—we can wait fifteen minutes at most."

"That won't be a problem. Rogers out."

He was running before the last word had left his mouth, sprinting through the trees and leaping over logs without breaking stride. Faster and faster he moved, wanting to leave the stink of burning narcotics and the even greater stench of corruption behind him. He tried not to think about the look of hopeless resignation in the eyes of the workers, or wonder how long it would be before they were back sorting and packaging illicit drugs. The workers probably didn't even spare a thought for the morality of what they were doing, and were just happy to be able to feed their families. The real villains—some of them a thousand miles away—were the ones making billions from the drug trade, and the politicians and law enforcement personnel pocketing bribes to look the other way. Steve's stride faltered for a moment.

So much corruption in this new world. Are we achieving anything with these little victories, or are they just pinpricks? What I wouldn't give for another war where I knew who the enemy was and what victory meant.

Steve couldn't help himself; he started laughing. He really was starting to sound like an old man yearning for the good old days. There'd been plenty of corruption back in his day—plenty of men living outside the law and exploiting the helpless. Today's enemy might not be as easily identified by their uniforms, but the fight remained the same. He could only hope that he had set the Ortega cartel back with this latest raid, and that with enough punishment, it would be forced to give up on its smuggling operation.

Steve burst into the clearing just as the Black Hawk

helicopter came into view above the treetops. Branches whipped in the downdraft from the rotating blades as the chopper slowly descended. It was still twenty feet above the ground when Steve leaped, grabbing the undercarriage with the poise of a circus acrobat before flexing his arms and flipping himself in through the open door, landing next to a startled Marine.

"Just thought I'd save you some time," Steve said.

The Marine nodded, his standard issue gyrene expression of unflappability already back in place.

"Yes, sir," he said, saluting.

Steve returned the salute.

"I'm Master Gunnery Sergeant Fischer, sir," he said, handing Steve an unmarked, white envelope. "I have a message for you."

Steve made no move to open it. "Who is it from?"

Fischer hesitated. "I can't tell you that, sir."

Rogers raised an eyebrow.

"You don't know?"

"I do know, sir."

"Then what's the problem?"

"I was asked to not to tell you, sir," the Marine said. "I owed the person a favor and they asked me to give this to you. My instructions were clear—straight into your hands only, no intermediaries, and no witnesses . . . and before we got back to base."

Steve stared at him.

"Marine, this is definitely not SOP," he said. "I don't like it one little bit."

"Yes, sir. Sorry, sir."

"What if I ordered you to tell me, Gunny?"

"I gave my word, sir," Fischer said stiffly.

"Well, I know better than to try and make a Marine break his word," Steve said. "And I wouldn't want to do something like that, even if I could."

"Thank you, sir," Fischer said. "I knew that of all people, you'd understand."

Steve tore the envelope open and scanned the single sheet of paper inside, trying to puzzle out the strange characters.

"You know, I'm sure I've seen this before. Not for a long time, back before the war."

"You're talking about the big one, right, sir? W-W-two?"

Steve suddenly felt very old. The man sitting across from him was a veteran, with grey temples and a grizzled face. But to him, Steve's yesterday was ancient history.

"That's right. Well, I can tell you right now that I'll need to get home before I can translate this."

"Well, sir, it's always nice to get home." Fischer's eyes took on a faraway look, as if he were suddenly in another place. "It's been a long time since I've been home."

"Me too, Marine. Me too."

* * *

S.H.I.E.L.D. had given Steve a nice place of his own. The lounge alone was as big as the apartment his whole family had shared when he was growing up, and sometimes he felt like a pea rattling around in a pod, barely making use of what, to him, seemed like luxury. But, he had made one room his own—the den. Its walls were covered in Second World War posters, and a cabinet that took up almost a whole wall held a huge transistor radio set that had been retrofitted with the latest in audio technology by a helpful technician back at the S.H.I.E.L.D. lab.

The entire room had an old-fashioned feel, and a man from the '30s would not have felt out of place sitting in there, which was the point. When Steve needed to think, this was where he came. Sitting in the comfortable leather chair at the desk, with a baseball game playing softly in the background, Steve found he could relax and consider his problems.

Lying on the desk in front of him, the white paper a stark contrast against the mellow oak, was the mysterious message. Steve had been staring at it for what seemed liked hours, trying to puzzle out where he had seen it before. The memory floated just on the edges of recollection, teasing him. He turned to the shelf of books and magazines at the side of the desk. Why did the message seem linked in his mind to those magazines? He rummaged through them—

it was a collection that would make any comic-book geek drool with envy. *Weird Tales. Amazing Stories. Astounding.* There! He pulled out a battered copy of *Galaxy*, then flipped through it, searching among the advertisements for X-ray glasses and sea monkeys for a half-forgotten memory. For a moment, he thought he'd picked up the wrong magazine, but there it was, in glorious color on the back.

STAR DECODER RING. Trade secret messages with your friends. Learn the amazing art of . . . STELLAR CRYPTOGRAPHY.

Steve reached into his desk drawer and pulled out the ring. It was only cheap plastic, but as an eleven-year-old, it had been his treasured possession. The ring worked on a simple substitution cipher, the circular face inscribed with a series of symbols that corresponded to a letter of the alphabet. The first word of the message would tell him which symbol equaled "a," and then solving the cipher would be merely a case of substituting the appropriate letter. The code was far from unbreakable, but its obscurity was such that anyone trying to break it would spend days trying to work out its origin, not believing that any code could be so simple. More importantly, Steve now knew with absolute certainty who the message was from, because no one else would have thought to use the ring.

Steve had been at one of the innumerable parties Tony Stark held at his luxurious Manhattan penthouse. He never really enjoyed Tony's get-togethers—they were completely alien to a young man who had grown up on the Lower East Side. He got on well enough with Tony, and the billionaire playboy had never made Steve feel like he thought less of Steve because of his humble background, but Rogers was very aware of their differences. He never knew what to talk about, or what one was meant to do at those kinds of events.

That night, he had been standing in the corner, awkwardly nursing a ginger ale and wondering when he could leave without being impolite, when Maria Hill had wandered over and started chatting with him. He wasn't sure, but he had gotten the feeling that she was as bored as he was. They didn't normally mingle much outside of what their jobs required—to say that they had a checkered history would be an understatement. But it was not in Steve's nature to be rude, and he was glad he'd given her a chance. They'd both been delighted to find that they shared a common interest in science fiction, especially of the pulp variety, and that this interest hadn't been ruined by their encounters with the real thing. They'd chatted about bug-eyed monsters for a good chunk of the night, and he had learned that one of the reasons Maria had ended up working for S.H.I.E.L.D. was because of a story she had read as child.

The invisible currents that made up Tony's parties had

swept them apart and Maria had been called over to a conversational circle where Tony was holding court, but Steve had been grateful for her easing his discomfort, enough so that when he had gotten home that night, he had dug through his magazines until he found the story that had had such an impact on her. When it had turned out that he owned two copies of that issue of *Galaxy*, he had sent her the second one. It had seemed like the nice thing to do, and part of him had hoped that their chat was a sign that they were both ready to forget some of the conflicts in their past and move on. He'd received a nice handwritten note in return, but that had been the end of it, and the whole episode had barely crossed his mind since.

Now, in his den, Steve leaned over the coded page and began to transcribe the message. At first, he needed to keep referring back to the ring, but he soon had the hang of it, and the words took shape with increasing speed. Finally done, he sat back with a frown creasing his classic, all-American features. Even decoded, the message was still cryptic and made little sense.

Dear Steve,
If you're reading this, you've remembered our conversation and know this is really me writing to you.
I'm sorry for the old-school secret agent routine, but I couldn't trust anything involving computers in

any way. Besides, I thought you of all people would appreciate this.

I need your help. We haven't always seen eye to eye, but I know that I can trust you to do what is right. That's the only thing I feel certain I can trust right now.

Below, you will see a set of coordinates—they are to an abandoned warehouse. I will be waiting there tomorrow at 1900 hours. I hope you will meet me so I can explain everything.

Please come alone—and trust NO ONE.

MH

No matter how many times Steve read the message, his confusion remained. Why was Maria Hill asking him for help? And, more importantly, who was she trying to hide her message from?

Chapter 2

Steve didn't skulk—there was nothing more suspicious than someone who was obviously sneaking around—but he did avoid the glare of the few streetlights that still lit up this less than affluent neighborhood. The trick to being invisible was to hide in plain sight, looking like you belonged, so that the casual eye just slid past you. He wore a shabby trench coat—liberated from a Salvation Army donation bin—over his distinctive uniform, and he walked slightly slouched to disguise his height and build. In this neighborhood, he was just another schmo down on his luck, not even worth the trouble of mugging.

As Steve got closer to his destination, the street traffic thinned out until, finally, he was alone. He looked around to be sure, then moved a manhole cover aside, the two hundred and fifty-pound piece of cast iron barely making him strain. He slipped underground and pulled the cover back into place above him. Fortunately, Steve was only in a storm drain; the city had long since started sending waste through a new piping system. Some things about the modern world were definitely an improvement. Still, the dank, stone-lined tunnel's stagnant water served as home to rats the size of small cats, and he couldn't help but be relieved when he'd covered the distance needed to arrive inside the warehouse's gate.

Steve emerged from the smell and the vermin into a shadowed alcove. There were a number of guards around the perimeter, all armed and wearing body armor. Their bulletproof vests bore no insignia, and Steve had no way of knowing whether the men were there with Maria, or whether they were the reason that she had taken so many precautions. Walking up and asking the men didn't seem like an option, so, silently, Rogers waited for his moment, then darted out of the alcove and into the warehouse, breathing a sigh of relief as the door clicked shut behind him without any sign he had been noticed.

The first few rooms inside were deserted offices, rats playing where secretaries had once typed, and their nests the only contents of abandoned in and out trays. Moving past a water cooler half full of a noisome green liquid, he came to a door marked *Loading Bay* and gently nudged it open, looking around carefully before stepping into a vast, open space. Steve had no idea what kind of business had been running in the warehouse, or what had been stored there, but all that remained was dust, debris, and few scattered desks and chairs. The space was almost a hundred feet across, and about forty feet to the ceiling, which was dotted with lights. Some of them still worked, casting a few pools of radiance into the eerie dimness.

Maria stood in one of the pools of light, for a moment looking like a statue of some ancient Greek goddess lit by moonlight. Then she turned and smiled, breaking the illusion. Instead of a chiton, she was wearing body armor and carrying a Glock 19 on each hip. Steve knew she could use them—he'd fought beside her and seen her put a cluster of bullets the size of her fist through her targets with each hand. Her dark hair was cut shorter than he remembered, but other than that, she hadn't changed at all since the last time he had seen her.

"Hello, Steve."

"Hello, Maria. You should know better than to stand in the brightest part of the room."

"I just wanted reassure you I was alone, Steve."

He walked toward her, keeping his hand on his shield and his eyes constantly scanning the shadows. He trusted Maria as much as he trusted anyone in S.H.I.E.L.D. these days, but that wasn't exactly a glowing recommendation.

"Are the guards meant to reassure me, too?"

"No, they're all about reassuring me," Maria said. "Don't worry, they have no idea why I'm here. I might trust them with my life, but there are very few people I trust with my secrets. Which is why you should feel really privileged. I'm about to tell you a big one."

"I feel very special," Steve said. "Nice work with the decoder ring, by the way."

"Thanks, I was rather proud of that one. I needed something that no one else would be able to identify—and something completely analog. Hard to come by these days."

"Analog?"

"As opposed to digital. We use computers for everything now, but I can't assume that they're secure." She smiled. "Plus, who doesn't want to use a secret decoder ring?"

Steve grabbed a couple of the less battered chairs scattered around the loading bay. Brushing them off, he positioned them in the pool of light. He waited for Maria to take a seat, then sat down across from her.

He noticed with surprise that Maria's hands were trembling slightly. She followed his gaze and flushed, clasping them in front of her to hide the shaking. The guards and the secrecy didn't concern Steve all that much, but seeing that Maria was actually scared shook him deeply. He'd seen her face firefights and board meetings with exactly the same expression—she was unflappably calm in every situation, and anything capable of frightening her was to be taken very seriously indeed. A creaking caught his attention, and looking down, he saw the arms of his chair flexing under his grip. With a conscious effort, he willed himself to relax, and turned his attention back to Maria.

"Maria, what are you so concerned about? We've had our differences, but you know that I'll do whatever I can to help."

Maria took a deep breath and brushed her dark hair back from her face. "It's that obvious?"

"Yes, it is."

"S.H.I.E.L.D. is a large organization. Alongside field operations and counter intelligence, we've got a massive research and development division, and we're always on the lookout for bright young minds to come and work for us. We take chances on people who don't fit in to the conventional mold that government agencies look for, and it's paying dividends. They keep us on the cutting edge—and a step ahead of some of the more established agencies that would happily see us shut down, or absorbed into their budgets."

Steve shrugged. He'd never cared for interdepartmental politics except when they got in his way. All he wanted to do was fight the bad guys. "Go on."

"A few years back, my cousin called me. We were close as children, and the only reason we had drifted apart was because of time and busyness, nothing more. She had a daughter who had just finished college and she was worried about her. All her daughter—Katherine, her name is—wanted was to work for the government. The problem was that Katherine might have been brilliant, but her genius came with a large dose of nonconformity, and she didn't fit in to the government's neat little boxes. She was rejected by all the normal agencies—the CIA, the FBI, the Shop. She was heartbroken, and her mother knew I worked somewhere in the government, though not where, of course."

"Of course."

"So, I read her résumé and interviewed her, and realized that the other agencies had missed out on something special. She really was a genius. There was nothing she couldn't get a computer to do. So I recruited her and put her to work in R and D. She didn't get any preferential treatment, and started out the same way that everyone else does. She had her normal projects, but we've lifted a page from the Google playbook and we give every tech a day a week to work on their own pet projects. Some of our most useful tools have come from that." Maria was talking quickly, the words coming out in a rapid fire.

"Maria, slow down and take your time."

With a visible effort of will, Maria took a deep breath and composed herself, sitting straighter in her chair.

"Anyway, one day I got a phone call from Katherine asking if she could meet me. I didn't think anything of it—we'd been talking about catching up for a while. But, when she arrived, well . . ." Maria trailed off.

"She was scared?" Steve asked.

"No!" Maria said. "She was furious. Absolutely incandescent with rage. It took me almost an hour and about three cosmopolitans to calm her down enough to get the story out of her."

"So what happened?"

"How much do you know about computers, Steve?"

"Not much. Just that the phone that Tony gave me is a thousand times more powerful than the computers that took up whole rooms at S.S.R. headquarters back in my day. Oh, and that people have a lot of kitten pictures."

"All true," Maria laughed. "But more than that, computers have become absolutely central to every aspect of our lives. They not only shape the way we view the world, they control it."

"Control it?" Steve frowned. "I'm not sure I like the sound of that."

"I wouldn't say I do either. But it's the way it is. We see the world through a screen, and it alters the way we perceive things."

"There are lots of good things about computers, though. When I first returned from my . . . Arctic holiday . . . I spent hours online trying to catch up. I couldn't believe how much information there was at my fingertips. If I'd had that in high school, I would have aced it. The only problem was filtering out all the noise and working out what was true and what was rubbish."

"Don't worry, that's not just a newbie problem."

"So, was that what Katherine was working on? A way of filtering the information?"

"No, but something even more valuable and dangerous. In the course of her research, she'd come across something that she said would revolutionize cryptography—that would change the way that information flowed across the internet."

"What was it?" Steve asked, then laughed. "Not that I would understand it. I won't lie, it took me fifteen hours just to work out how to turn on my computer the first time I used it."

"Steve, we have limited time, and I'm not going to waste it by taking you through the evolution of computing. I'm not trying to be rude, but it's really not important right now."

"Fair enough," Steve said. "I'm guessing the important part is what she told you that's left you so rattled."

Maria took a deep breath. "Katherine said that when she reported her findings to her supervisor, he told her to cease research immediately and forget she'd ever come up with the idea. When she protested, she was called in to the head of her department's office and raked over the coals. Threatened with termination or exile to some remote office in Hicksville."

"And she quit?" Steve asked.

"No. She may have a temper, but she's smart enough to hide it when she has to. She stood and took the tongue-lashing, and then called me the next day. She wanted to know what I thought she should do."

"And what did you tell her?"

"To keep her head down and do what she was told, of course." Steve almost believed Maria for a second, then saw the mischievous glint in her eye. "No. I told her I would look into it, quietly, but she should just go about her work as if she'd learned her lesson."

"Sneaky," Steve said, admiration in his voice. "This is why I'm no good at this stuff. Just point me at a problem and I'll deal with it, but anything more than that, and I get all confused."

"Oh, don't play the hayseed with me, Steve," Maria said. She was shaking her head, but he could see that he was succeeding in distracting her from her concerns. A little, anyway. "You've been doing this a lot longer than I have."

"I guess so. But even if I hadn't, like I said before—it's obvious you're scared. Why?"

"Once I'd spoken to Katherine, I started investigating. It's not that I don't trust her, but the first thing I did was try and verify her claims. I managed to get access to her personal computer, but her files were gone—more than gone; it was as if they had never existed."

"But something convinced you," Steve said. "Or we wouldn't be here."

"My next step was checking the files on the systems of her

supervisor and department head. If her research was every-thing she had claimed, and they had killed it, not only had they exceeded their authority, but something was really wrong—either gross incompetence or something more sinister. Either way, I felt it was something that needed to be looked into. But it was the same story—no evidence of her research. But this was when I realized that I was onto something. It wasn't just that there was no research—there was nothing at all."

"What do you mean?" Steve asked, puzzled.

"There was nothing else from Katherine on their machines. She had to have been producing something, or she wouldn't have been employed for long. If I'd found the normal stuff, regular work projects and the like, I wouldn't have been suspicious. But her whole file had been expunged. That was enough to set my alarms off."

"So what did you do?"

"It put me in awkward position. I had no evidence other than her claims, but I'm sure they could have explained away the missing files and it would have been their word against hers. I would have been laughed at if I tried to launch an official investigation. It may not be the 1940s but the boys' clubs haven't disappeared completely."

"What was your next step, then?" Steve asked.

"It was taken out of my hands. I like to think that I'm pretty good at covering my tracks, but someone must have worked out what I was up to."

"What makes you say that?" Steve asked.

"It was little things at first. Last accessed dates on computer files changed, drawers in my office slightly askew. Then I started feeling like I was being followed. Whoever they were, they were very good, and I couldn't prove it. But you know that feeling you get, that someone is tailing you?"

Maria gave Steve a defiant look, as if daring him to say that it was merely her imagination. Steve did no such thing; he knew exactly what she meant. In fact, that same feeling had saved his life on several occasions.

"Did you report anything?" Steve asked.

"No, all I had were suspicions. And, Steve, you're missing something. Something important."

He thought for a moment. "Sorry, you'll have to help me out."

She leaned forward. "Steve, you know how close I am to the top at S.H.I.E.L.D. There are very few people who have access to my office when I'm not around, or who could infiltrate my computer system. It has to have been someone on the inside. Not just the inside of S.H.I.E.L.D., but in my department. Even if Katherine's superiors are traitors, they don't have that level of access, so there has to be someone else."

Steve frowned. "Hydra?"

"I doubt it. We've been extra vigilant since the . . . unpleasantness," Maria said. "There are certain traits we now know to look for, common elements that we know to watch for. And, even if it was Hydra, we have protocols in place so that another bulk infiltration of the agency would be almost impossible. But one or two people in the right place—that's much harder to guard against, and there's still a capacity for a great deal of damage."

"Maria, you're still holding back something. I can understand you being scared for Katherine, but it's obvious there's something else, something more personal."

"When I really started to get worried was when I came home to find that someone had been in my house, Steve. I've gone to great lengths to make sure there is no record of my real address. No one should know where I live. No one. Not even Nick knows." Steve almost flinched at the raw fury in her voice, and she continued. "That place is my sanctuary from all this. Knowing that someone had intruded on that is an awful feeling. By the time this is over, someone will be very sorry for that."

Maria paused before speaking again. "That's one thing, but there's something else—I'm almost certain someone is trying to kill Katherine." Her tone was so matter of fact that Steve almost missed the import of her words. "Again, nothing I can prove. She was waiting for the subway, during peak hour, and someone jostled her. She fell on the tracks but someone pulled her up just in time."

"But it could have been an accident?" Steve asked.

"Once could have been an accident, but there have been other incidents. It's starting to look like a pattern."

"So you want me to find out who's behind this?"

"No." She held up a hand to cut him off. "I know that isn't your skill set, Steve. I'm going to keep digging and see what turns up."

"So what do you need from me?" He was pretty sure he knew.

"I need time, but I don't know how much of that I have. There are only so many accidents one person can walk away from. I need you to keep Katherine alive so I can focus on finding out who wants her dead."

"Surely you have resources who are better suited for a bodyguard job," Steve said. "It's not that I don't want to help, but I'm not sure I'm the best man for the task."

"Don't be obtuse, Steve. You're the *only* man for the job. At the moment, I don't know who I can trust inside the organization. There might only be one more traitor working with the two that I suspect, but as yet, I haven't even been able to narrow it down to a list of possibilities. What if I chose the one person I shouldn't have, and Katherine died because of my mistake? At this point, I really only have one guarantee—no one has ever questioned your integrity." Maria smiled, and it was little less forced than the others had been, a little closer to the real thing. "And let's be honest, who's going to try going through you to get to her?"

Maria must have seen the hesitancy in his face.

"Please, Steve. I need your help. Katherine needs your help." Maria played her trump card. "You aren't going to leave her defenseless, are you?"

"That's a dirty trick, Maria." There wasn't any heat in his voice. She had him, and they both knew it. He could never resist an appeal to his sense of responsibility. Looking out for people was what he did. More importantly, if he said no and anything happened to Katherine, he would never forgive himself, even if he'd never met the girl.

"Fine, where is she?"

Maria passed Steve a scrap of paper with an address on it, grabbing his hand and squeezing it hard, her eyes locked on his and burning with intensity.

"She's in a safe house—one that hasn't been integrated into the network yet, and that I'm pretty sure no one but me and one or two others know about. It's the best I can do, but I don't know how long it will be safe for. I'm scared for her every moment that she's alone," Maria said. She let go of his hand, her touch lingering on his jacket sleeve for a few moments. "Get her out of the city while I lay a false trail to make it look like she's out of the country. I'll fake plane tickets, customs clearances—the works."

Steve nodded. "I know a place I can take her. A friend of

mine who has the gift of discretion owes me a favor. Most importantly, there's no connection with any of the agencies. And then what?"

"Give me a week; by then, I should know more. Then bring her back to the city—it will be the last place anyone will be looking for her, plus I need to be here while I chase information, so I'll want her close to hand when I find something. Find somewhere to lay low where I can reach you and wait for word from me. Can you do that?"

"Don't worry, Maria, I'll keep her safe," Steve said. "But you need to look out for yourself, too."

"Don't worry about me, Rogers, I can take care of myself. You just keep Katherine safe for me."

"I will. I promise," he said.

"That's all I wanted to hear. If you can't trust Captain America's word, whose can you trust?"

With that, Maria turned and walked toward the exit without looking back. Steve stared after her for a moment, hoping that she wasn't heading into more danger than she could handle. But then he caught himself—when it came to Maria Hill, it was more likely that anyone getting in her way would be the one in danger.

Chapter 3

The safe house looked like just any other suburban home, right down to the abandoned tricycle that sat on the lawn next to a discarded ball. Anyone walking past would have simply thought it was occupied by a family with a dog and 2.5 kids, too busy to mow their lawn quite as often as they should, but otherwise completely unremarkable. That was what made it a good safe house. Of course, the average citizen wouldn't have noticed the ring of masked men surrounding the building. Some were positioned on rooftops, others in the shadowy paths that ran between homes. Steve was grateful to the instinct that had prompted him to dump his motorcycle a few blocks back.

Biding his time with the patience bred by a thousand ambushes, Steve trudged around the block, giving the appearance of aimless wandering until he had mapped out all of the watchers' locations in his mind. He'd kept the battered trench coat on, hoping that any observers would simply assume he was another homeless man in a city full of them. There was only one place that wasn't overlapped by at least two of the watchers—a narrow path that ran between the safe house and one of its neighbors. He assumed that had been one of the reasons that the safe house had been chosen, as the path provided a means of escape if worse came to worst.

The side yard of the safe house was shielded by the spread branches of a row of willows, the shadows growing as the sun traced its weary way across the sky. He had about an hour until it was fully dark, and Steve guessed that that was when the men would make their move—it was what he would have done.

Once he was sure that he had located all of the observers, Steve slipped down the path between the houses. The watcher in this area was halfway up one of the trees, concealed among the branches. His camouflage was the latest in stealth tech, and he was nearly indistinguishable from the shadows that moved across him as the leaves shifted with the wind. The observer himself was almost completely motionless; the only thing that had betrayed him was a brief moment when he had flinched, as if bitten by a bug or a spider. Even with that giveaway, Steve had nearly lost the watcher again several times. Slinking along the fence behind the tree, Steve reached down and picked up a large rock, then straightened and hurled it at the man in one fluid motion. Stunned, the man toppled from the tree, and Steve made short work of him, leaving him unconscious and bound to the trunk. Steve had searched him for a clue as to who had sent him, but the man was a ghost, completely free of identifying insignia. Even the labels on his clothing had been removed.

Rogers now moved with fresh urgency. He knew it was only a matter of time before the man was discovered and the place swarmed with backup. Prying off one of the side-fence palings, he squeezed through and into the yard of the safe house, keeping low to the ground and staying in the shadows. Steve froze, his face mere inches away from a gleaming trip wire. He had no idea who might be in the house, and whether it was already compromised. Setting off any alarms, silent or otherwise, would hardly help his cause—he didn't know whether the watchers had tapped the phone lines and would be able to intercept the alarm, and know that someone else was in the area.

Carefully, he stepped over the wire and, keeping low as he moved to avoid any unfriendly eyes, finally made it to the basement door at the side of the house. He ran his hands along the doorframe, finding the seam where the locking mechanism met the frame. Steve pulled a small, rectangular square about the size of a credit card, but made of steel, from his pocket. Slowly, he worked it into the gap between the lock and the frame, jiggling it back and forth until he heard the soft click of the latch sliding back into the faceplate. Steve opened the door and checked it carefully for pressure pads or wires, before slipping into the basement, careful not to make any noise.

It was a perfectly normal looking basement, empty of any decoration, and with no sign of motion detectors or cameras. In the corner, a set of stairs led up into the house; he quickly climbed them and found himself in a narrow hallway illuminated by bright lighting. Placing his feet with a delicacy that anyone would have been surprised to see in such a big man, he made his way silently toward the main living area, ignoring the closed doors to either side of that room. The sound of canned laughter from a TV sitcom floated toward him, and Steve made sure his shield was positioned perfectly on his back in case it was needed.

Steve stepped into the living area and froze. The light was off, the only illumination coming from the flickering images on the television screen. The chair in front of the television was empty, rocking slightly as if it had been occupied only a moment before. A faint whisper of movement came from behind him and Steve turned—straight into a punch that landed flush on his chin. He shook his head slightly, shaking off the pain, and raised his arm to ward off the next blow.

His assailant was outlined by the light from the hall, and he could make out the slender silhouette of a figure that barely came up to his shoulder. Whoever it was, they were fast, unleashing a flurry of blows that had surprising power for the size of the attacker. Steve managed to keep most of the blows from landing, but he was handicapped by a desire not to cause any damage in return. He was uncertain of who his assailant was, and he was conscious of the fact that he was, after all, the intruder here. He grunted as a small fist struck him under the ribs; this was followed by a knee headed straight to his groin that he just managed to twist fast enough away from to catch on the big muscle of his leg.

"Okay, that's enough. That could have been painful."

He caught the next punch in his gauntleted hand and squeezed hard enough that bones creaked. His attacker let out a gasp as Steve bent the captured wrist back, causing them both to fall to their knees. The light from the television flared, revealing the face of a young girl—no, a young woman, early twenties at the most. Steve was so surprised that he almost missed the flash of metal from the pistol she was bringing up with her free hand. A moment later, the gun flew across the room as he chopped the inside of her wrist with the rigid blade of his hand.

"Ouch! That hurt."

The indignation in her voice left Steve speechless for a second.

"What did you expect, me to let you shoot me?"

"It would have been nice of you," she snapped.

Steve chuckled at the ridiculousness of that, then shot out his hand to catch the fist flying toward him.

"Will you stop that," he said irritably. "I'm not here to hurt you."

"Funny way of showing it."

"I could have hurt you if I'd wanted to," Steve said patiently. "Surely you know that."

"I know no such thing. And I don't know you, either. Why should I believe anything you say?"

As she spoke, the young woman strained against Steve's grip, her muscles quivering with effort. She may as well have been trying to bend a steel bar for all the success she was having, but he had to admire her determination.

"Look, you may not know me, but I know you must be Katherine, and you know the person who sent me. Maria asked me to take care of you."

She froze in his grip.

"Aunt Maria sent you? You're friends?"

"I'd like to think we have a mutual respect for each other, but we aren't BFFs or anything." Steve was rather proud of himself for remembering what modern youth said. "She said to remind you about the yellow chrysanthemums, whatever that means."

Katherine relaxed slightly, and Steve let go of her hand. She stood, and Steve watched her warily as she brushed herself off, just in case she had ideas about launching another attack. Instead, she plopped into the armchair and grabbed the television remote, flicking through the channels.

"They're my mom's favorite flowers. Still, if you'd claimed that you were . . . BFFs, then I would have known not to trust you, code word or not." The pause told Steve that he hadn't impressed her with his attempt at being modern. "I don't think Aunt Maria is the sort of person to have a BFF."

"She's a good woman," Steve said with a hint of reproach in his voice.

"Oh, don't get me wrong. I love her dearly, and she's always been very kind to me. She's just . . . reserved, I guess you'd call it."

Steve nodded. Reserved was a good choice of word when it came to Maria.

"And now I recognize you, too. You look a little different out of your uniform, but you're Captain America, aren't you? I've seen you on TV, and once at headquarters. You were with Tony Stark, and they were giving you both a tour of the new armory. We couldn't believe we were seeing you in the flesh."

"We're just like anyone else," he said, slightly embarrassed. He hoped he wasn't going to be dealing with a case of hero worship. Her next words quickly dispelled that notion.

"Tony really is hot." She looked at him. "He doesn't seem like a square, either."

"Tony's a good guy," Steve said. "We have the occasional . . . difference of opinion, but we're on the same side."

"Don't take this the wrong way, but from what I've seen,

you seem like someone who's big on rules and regulations. You know . . . the military background and all."

"Rules are there for a reason, most of the time," Steve said defensively. "Tony and I disagree about that occasionally, but that doesn't stop us from being friends."

"Are you BFFs?" It took him a moment to realize that she was teasing him.

"Look, we really have to get out of here," Steve said. "There are some people watching the house, and I don't think they're here to check on your well-being."

"So you say. You can go if you want; I was just about to make some soup," Katherine said. "You can have some if you promise not to twist my arm again."

Steve followed Katherine into the kitchen, and pulled up a stool while she busied herself among the cupboards. It took a great deal of willpower not to simply grab her and bundle her out of the house, but he knew if he did that, it would be the end of her trusting him, and if he was going to keep her safe, he would need her cooperation. Forcing her from the house would have to be a last resort, so, instead, he gritted his teeth and watched as she pulled out a large pot and placed it on the stove. He'd give her five minutes, and then he would have to make a decision—and deal with the consequences.

"How does tomato sound?"

"Fine with me," Steve said. "But once you've had something to eat, we need to make a move."

"Whoa, hang on a moment. Who said I was coming with you?"

"What do you mean? Why wouldn't you? We've established that I do know Maria, and that she was the one who sent me. Not to mention, this safe house is no longer safe."

"That's not the point, Cap— what do I call you? I'm not calling you Captain America."

"Steve is fine," he said impatiently. "So, what is the point?"

"Steve, the problem is that you're as establishment as they come. I mean, you carry around a flag wherever you go, for crying out loud!"

"And what's wrong with that?" Steve asked stiffly. "I'm proud to wear that emblem, and to carry it on my shield. Why wouldn't I be?"

"I hate to tell you this, Steve, but this country isn't always in the right."

"I think it's more often right than not."

"I wish I felt the same way," Katherine said. "I've been working for the government for the last two years, and look where I am now—the government isn't always your friend. It's certainly not mine at the moment, anyway. And you don't get much more government than Captain America."

"It's obviously rogue elements, but that doesn't mean everyone is against you."

"For rogue elements they seem pretty well informed. Aunt Maria told me that they knew where she lived," Katherine said. "And it isn't just that. It's not the first time I've been told to stop pursuing avenues of research that have the potential to make a huge difference for a lot of people. The moment an issue is bigger than just one country, they can't look past partisan self-interest. Sometimes, I think they forget that they're meant to work for the people, not the other way around."

Steve couldn't argue with that. He'd seen too much of it himself—people in politics or public service for themselves, not out of any sense of patriotism or duty. Still, he wasn't sure it was fair to tar everyone with the same brush.

"Maybe they had their reasons," Steve said. "We don't always know the big picture, and we can get caught up in our little corner of it."

"Don't patronize me," Katherine snapped. "I'm not a child. I know the difference between a bit of caution and something more sinister. Anyway, it was the moment I told my supervisor about my project that things got really weird. He has to be part of it."

"If you're going to keep us sitting here while we wait for whoever's outside to decide what to do, can you at least tell me about this project? Maria was very hazy on the details," Steve said. "I've got no clue about the specifics."

"Why do you want to know?" Katherine asked suspiciously. "It's one thing telling Aunt Maria, but just because my superiors are stupid, or corrupt, it doesn't mean I'm going to start spilling state secrets. It may sound silly to you, but I'm hoping to still a have a career after this. Working in that lab was a dream come true for me."

"If I'm going to protect you, the more I know, the better," Steve said. "That's all."

"I don't know whether I can trust you." Katherine stared at him defiantly. "Until I do—if I ever do—I won't be telling you anything."

"Hang on a minute!" Steve said angrily. "Why don't you trust me? Are you implying I'm part of this . . . conspiracy against you, or whatever it is? If so, I resent that."

"No, I guess I can trust Maria's judgment on that. Plus, I don't think you're capable of helping have someone knocked off."

"Then what is it?"

She gave him a considering look, as if trying to decide whether to elaborate.

"It's obvious we have very different opinions about the wisdom of our government. I have to be honest, I'm bit worried that if I do tell you, you'll feel duty bound to confiscate my research, or try and shut it down for the good of the nation, or some sort of rubbish like that."

Steve was more than angry now.

"The good of the nation isn't rubbish. But I gave Maria my word I would keep you alive, and the only way I'll break that promise is if someone kills me first."

"Keep me alive. Not keep me free, right?" Katherine said.

"It's what you might do for my own good that worries me."

"I think you're being a bit harsh given that you barely know me," Steve said. He took a deep breath and tried to remember how young she was, and that she was likely scared to death and trying to hide it. "I don't know what I can say to put you at ease."

"Neither do I," she replied. "So that puts us in an awkward position, doesn't it?"

Steve nodded. "It does. How about this? I won't insist on learning your secret if you come with me. Now."

She started to protest, but he cut her off.

"I'm not saying you need my protection. But it will make me feel much better, and let me keep my promise to Maria. If you don't need me, then that's fine, but at least I get to feel useful. Sound fair?"

"I guess so."

Although she had said it grudgingly, Steve could see the relief on her face. It had been pride stopping her from accepting his help, and he'd given her a way to back down while still saving face.

"So, can I ask one more favor?" he asked.

"Depends what it is."

"I've been doing this for a while, so if we do happen to come under attack or anything like that, will you follow my lead?"

"I'm not stupid. I'm a genius when it comes to computers, but I know my limitations. If it's a situation that you're better at dealing with, I'll listen."

"That's very reasonable of you," Steve said. "I appreciate it."

"Look, I don't . . ."

Whatever she was about to say was cut off by the sound of smashing glass coming from all parts of the house. This was followed by splintering wood and the sound of booted feet on the floors.

Chapter 4

Steve was up and moving when the kitchen door slammed open. A small ovoid object came sailing through the door, but his hand was already on the handle of the pot sitting on the stove. With a backhand motion, he swatted the object, sending it flying back the way it had come.

"Cover your ears and close your eyes!"

A shout of alarm came from outside, followed by a jarring noise and a bright flash.

"Flash grenade," Steve said to Katherine. "Head down to the basement and don't come up, no matter what. If I'm not there in five minutes, make a run for it. Not a minute more, or less. Got it?"

"But what about you?" Katherine asked. "I can help."

"I'll be fine, but I can't watch out for myself and for you at the same time. Now, GO!"

As Katherine headed toward the basement stairs, Steve sprinted out the kitchen door, running low and fast. Three men were scattered in the hallway, two lying prone. The other had pulled himself to his knees, but was busy vomiting, the flash grenade having done its work all too well. He barely reacted before Steve was on him, a knee to his head sending him to join his companions on the ground.

Steve followed the sound of footsteps on the other side of the wall, and then turned, driving his shoulder into the drywall, hard. He crashed through into the living room, sending another pair of intruders flying. Two punches and they were out. The third man was short, giving up almost a foot to Steve, but broad across the shoulders, with the appearance of an ambulatory fire hydrant. Like the rest of the intruders, he wore a black uniform bare of any insignia or identifying marks, but he carried two short staves strapped to his back, each about three feet long. At the sight of Steve, he pulled them from their sheaths with an ease that spoke of long practice. He walked slowly toward Steve, staves spinning in long, looping patterns.

"I've always wanted to see how good you were," the man said softly. "I'd love to be the man who took Captain America down, even if I'm the only one who knows about it." There was something familiar about the voice, but Steve couldn't quite place it. Then the man attacked, and, fighting for his life, Steve didn't have any more time for thinking.

For all his squat stature, the man was fast. Before Steve could pull his shield from his back, one of the staves was arcing toward his head. Rogers caught it on his forearm and, despite the padding built in to his sleeve, felt the shock of the blow all the way to the bone. Whatever wood the weapons were made of, it was strong; the force of that blow should have snapped the stave clean in half.

All this went through Steve's mind in a heartbeat. By the time the second stave was whistling toward his ribs, his shield was in its path. The other man cursed as he lost his balance, the momentum of the stave so completely absorbed by the shield's Vibranium that it fell from his grasp. The stave skittered across the floor, coming to a rest against the wall.

Steve's attacker didn't let the loss of one of his weapons distract him; the other was already swinging toward Steve's head. This time Rogers caught it, the wood landing in his palm with a meaty smack. With a hard yank, he pulled the other man toward him, rapping his opponent across the bridge of the nose with his shield. Steve's assailant staggered back, blood pouring from his face, and Rogers followed with a roundhouse kick to the man's temple. His eyes rolled up into the back of his head and he collapsed in a boneless heap.

Even before the man had hit the floor, Steve was spinning to face the other entrance to the room. He brought his shield up just in time block the volley of bean bag rounds fired from the shotguns the pair of intruders charging toward him were holding. Steve continued his momentum, the rim of his shield catching one man under the ribs, then cracking into the temple of the other. Steve made a mental note that whoever these men were, they were here to capture Katherine, not kill her. He hadn't seen a single lethal weapon yet, but he knew that even bean bag rounds and truncheons could kill if luck ran against you. And even when people had been ordered to take someone alive, accidents sometimes happened in the heat of battle.

He did another sweep of the house. All of the intruders were unconscious or incapacitated, but he knew that more would be coming. And now that they knew there was more than one person in the house, the gloves might come off. He ran down into the basement, ducking under the flowerpot that Katherine hurled at his head the moment he came into her eye line.

"Sorry, I thought—"

"It's okay. You've got a pretty good arm, by the way."

He ran over to her, then looked out the basement windows and up into the yard.

"We have to get out of here. We don't have much time."

"Where are we going?" Katherine asked.

"Never mind that now," Steve said, trying not to snap at her. She was putting on a brave face, but he knew that she had to be scared. "We need to get past the perimeter before we do anything else."

Katherine didn't look happy about it, but she followed him out the basement door. They snuck through the shadows, no longer worrying about trip wires or alarms, and darted through the space between the houses. The observer that Steve had dealt with earlier was gone; he guessed that that was what had triggered the raid. He kept his eyes out for more attackers, but, for now at least, the coast was clear. In fact, the streets were eerily deserted; there was no foot traffic at all, and no sounds came from the houses around them. Windows were shuttered and blinds were closed, and no lights burned through the cracks. Steve led Katherine to where he had hidden his motorcycle, and dragged it out onto the footpath. Jumping on, he beckoned her to join him. She hesitated for a moment, then swung her leg over the pillion and took her place behind him. He kicked the machine to life, and they took off with a squeal of burning rubber.

Three blocks later, just as he was starting to think they might have made it past the perimeter unnoticed, he realized they were being followed. As the pair of headlights behind them was joined by another, Steve swung onto a path between two houses where a car couldn't follow. Their pursuers were a step ahead, though; he could hear the sound of motorcycles behind him, and then the drumming beat of helicopter blades above. He pulled through a yard and back out onto the road, and was immediately flanked by two motorcycles, the riders clad in black and their helmets giving the impression of monstrous insects. One of the riders pulled a long-barreled revolver from his jacket and pointed it at Steve. Before Rogers could react, Katherine kicked out and connected with the side of the other motorcycle. The rider dropped the gun to wrestle with the handlebars, trying to keep his balance. But the wobble proved too much, and he careened off the road into the bushes. The second motorcyclist swerved closer, trying to grab at Katherine. Steve didn't know what the man was thinking—maybe he had lost his head in the excitement of the chase—but there was no way that anyone could transfer a struggling hostage to the back of a moving motorcycle.

Katherine rendered the chain of thought moot, grabbing Steve's shield and neatly clotheslining the other rider. The shield connected with the rider's helmet with a nasty thunk, and he went flying backward, tumbling end over end before coming to rest in a heap in the middle of the road. The man's motorcycle kept going for a few hundred feet before teetering over and smashing into the curb with a very satisfying crunch of glass and metal.

"Very nice," Steve yelled.

"Thanks!"

The road had opened up now, with fewer houses to either side. Two cars were coming up behind them, fast, and Steve blinked against the glare of the bright spotlight lancing through the sky from the chopper above them.

"Hang on, this could get interesting," he yelled to Katherine. "Let's see if we can shake them off."

"Shake them off? How?"

As they came around a curve, a beautiful vista opened before them. They were on the side of a hill, and below them the city was laid out like a child's railway set. The hill was terraced, each level covered with houses and, to their left, the roadside dropped off, revealing rooftops just below. Rogers made a quick mental calculation of the distance and the weight of the motorcycle with the two riders. He didn't like the way the numbers came up, but he was running out of options.

"Hold on tight!" Steve yelled.

He revved the engine as hard as he dared, building up speed before he swerved, launching the bike out over the drop. Katherine's arm tightened convulsively around his waist as they plummeted toward the rooftops, wheels spinning as they searched for traction in thin air. Steve lifted the front wheel as the rear came down with a thump on the peak of a roof, then eased the front wheel back down. The bike shuddered, and for a moment Steve thought they were going to tip over, but he somehow held the bike steady as they raced along the rooftop. The houses were built close together and, after the insane leap to the first rooftop, merely keeping the bike going from house to house seemed easy. Katherine was screaming something in his ear, but it was lost in the roar of the wind in his ears.

"I can't hear you!"

"I said, 'are you crazy?'!" she screamed.

"Nope, I just enjoy a bit of a nighttime ride. Hold on."

Up ahead, there was a garden shed with a roof that sloped down almost to the ground, and Steve revved the engine as he jumped the bike off of the roof and rode down the side of the makeshift ramp before pulling back onto the road. They'd lost the cars in the plunge off the hill, but still had the helicopter to worry about. There were no trees to speak of, but ahead a string of power lines crossed the road and continued into a flat, grassy field. Steve drove beneath the lines and then turned off the road once more, following the line of wires while swerving around the poles, weaving in and out. The helicopter followed, staying well above the lines, the light cutting through the night to follow their passage. The power lines cast strange, skeletal shadows across the field, adding to the unreality of the situation and making it hard for Steve to find clear ground.

Up ahead, Steve could see a fence that marked where the field met the woods. He knew if he could make it under the cover of the trees he could lose the chopper, but it was clear that his pursuers were thinking the same thing. As Steve and Katherine drew closer to the fence and its fragile promise of safety, the whine of the helicopter's blades changed pitch. The chopper came in as close to the wires as the pilot dared, and there was a sound like a giant swatch of fabric being torn in two. As heavy machine-gun rounds hit the ground, a line of dirt fountained up alongside the motorcycle, first on one side, then on the other. Steve ignored it as best he could, continuing toward the fence line, but the next eruption of dirt was right in front of them. He swerved hard to the right, then back to the left, cutting a zigzag pattern across the field. Each time he tried to get closer to the woods, the fearful noise of the twin-mounted Gatling-type miniguns filled the night air, and another wall of dirt was thrown up into the air. Finally, fed up with the pursuit, Steve yanked the bike around hard, the wheels skidding before he regained control and sent them hurtling back toward the helicopter.

"Reach around and take the handlebars," he shouted to Katherine.

"What? No!" she screamed back. "What are you going to do?"

"Just do it!"

Ignoring her protests, Steve grabbed her hands and placed them on the handlebars, pressing down until he felt her grip them. Without another word, he scrambled to his feet, balancing precariously on the pillion. As they passed under the chopper, he leaped straight up, grabbing the landing gear. He swung back and forth a few times, then used his momentum to flip up through the open door. This time, instead of a startled Marine, there were two black-clad men and a gunner staring at him with dumbfounded expressions. The frozen tableau held for a moment, then shattered as the nearest man launched himself from his seat, a wicked foot-long knife appearing in his hand as if by magic. Rogers grabbed his attacker's wrist and turned slightly, using the man's momentum to help him on his way straight through the open door and to the ground below. The helicopter had come in low enough that Steve could see him struggling to sit up.

The second man was either more experienced or less rash. Instead of risking getting within reach of Rogers, the assailant went for the gun holstered at his side. He was very fast, but Rogers brought up his shield in time to block the two shots the man got off—and this time they weren't bean bag rounds. Steve didn't give the man a chance to fire again; the rim of the shield caught him under the chin and left him slumped in his harness. The gunner was scrabbling at his own harness, trying to free himself. By the time he managed to unclasp the buckle at his waist, Steve had his arm cocked and was ready to hurl his shield. The gunner looked at Steve, and then at the open door. Steve winked and nodded toward the opening. The gunner sighed, then threw himself into the air.

Steve made his way to the front of the helicopter. Leaning over the front seats, he rapped his fist against the side of the pilot's helmet, getting his attention.

"Land it. Now."

The pilot froze, then shrugged. "Whatever you say, boss. They don't pay me enough to argue with you."

He pushed the joystick forward and brought the helicopter down gently next to the two fallen men. At a nod from Steve, he flicked the switches that shut down the machine. After the noise of the chopper, the sudden silence was strange in Steve's ears. The quiet was broken by the sound of a motorcycle, but he relaxed when he recognized the familiar notes of an engine he had stripped down, bored out, and built back up a hundred times. He turned back to the pilot and spread his hands apologetically.

"You've been so obliging, and I hate to do this to you, but . . ."

Quickly, but gently, he tied the pilot to his chair, pulling his arms back behind the seat and securing them with the man's own belt. A few minutes later, he was dragging the other men back into the chopper. They'd come prepared, and their belts had a number of restraints to choose from, from standard police-issue handcuffs to nylon zip ties. Steve took a perverse pleasure in using their own tools against them. All three men—including the knife man, who was still out cold—were too stunned from the drop to put up any resistance.

Job finished, Steve jumped out of the chopper and trotted over to where Katherine had pulled up on the bike.

"Well, that was a bit dramatic, wasn't it?" she said.

"Maybe, but effective enough. Let's get out of here."

"What are you waiting for?"

Steve coughed. "Are you going to let me back on?"

"Sure, but why do you get to drive? Is it because you're the man? That's not a very good attitude."

"Ah, no—it's because I know where we're going, and you don't."

She deflated slightly.

"You make a good point." She shifted back on the seat, making room for him. "Hop on. But, can you do me a favor?"

He raised one eyebrow.

"Next time you're about to ride over a cliff onto a roof, can you give me some warning?"

Steve grinned at her. "No promises."

Chapter 5

The mountain air was cool and crisp, and Steve savored the feeling of the breeze blowing through his sweat-tangled hair as he removed his helmet. They had been riding for the better part of the day, and even his augmented muscles were complaining. He could only imagine what Katherine must be feeling, but, to her credit, she hadn't complained of any soreness. Of course, she had complained about a lot other things, from Steve's unwillingness to share their destination to the limited food options along the way. Steve had been able to use the excuse of road noise to ignore most of it, and as they had traveled, she had gradually quieted, lost in her own introspective thoughts.

By the time the remaining pursuers had arrived at the field, Steve and Katherine were already in the woods outside the city. They had little trouble following back roads out to a highway, and Steve had only stopped once, to make a call from a phone booth at a service station and to fuel up.

After that, it had just been miles and miles of open road, the countryside slowly changing as their altitude increased. The trees had thinned out, and nothing stood between the travelers and the breathtaking views of the valleys around them. From time to time, Steve would pull over, giving the excuse that he needed to stretch his legs. They both knew it was so that they could take in the view, but Katherine didn't say anything.

"So, are you going to tell me where we're going?" Katherine asked, interrupting Steve's enjoyment of the latest view. "Are we at least close? My butt fell asleep about a hundred miles ago, and I'm scared it will never wake up."

"Yeah, it's only a few miles farther," Steve replied. "It's nice; you'll like it."

They hopped back on the motorcycle and continued along the road, the mountain leveling out to a wide plateau. They kept going until they came to a narrow driveway. Steve carefully followed it as it wound up the slope, until it finally came out into a broad clearing that overlooked a valley. The view was exquisite; Steve could see immediately why the original builder had chosen this location. The valley stretched out for miles, trees hugging its curves, and far below he could see the sapphire ribbon of a swift-flowing river. The cabin itself was simple but well built out of roughly hewn logs so cunningly fitted together that not a single gap could be seen between them. The roof was shingled with dark slate and boasted a rather large number of solar panels. Several water tanks were positioned to either side of the house, and a satellite dish was mounted on the eave.

Behind the house was a well-tended vegetable garden, fenced off with chicken wire and metal stakes. A mix of plants grew in it—tomatoes and lettuce, as well as herbs and spices, and a battered scarecrow watched over all of them with one beady eye. On the other side of the garden, Katherine could make out a large shed with more solar panels on its roof. The whole place had an air of being well cared for, and all of the materials were good quality, right down to the expensive lock on the shed door.

"Wow, your friend is very thorough," Katherine said. "Looks like he has all his bases covered. What is he, some sort of survivalist?"

"No, he just doesn't like having to rely on anyone," Steve replied.

"Including the power companies, I take it?"

"Anyone."

"Well, looks like he doesn't have to. How long can we stay?"

"As long as we want to," Steve said. "But we'll be doubling back to the city in a week or so to get in touch with your aunt."

"You must have done this guy one big favor!"

"He thinks so. I thought I was just doing the right thing."

Katherine looked over at him, an unreadable expression on her face. "You really are a big Boy Scout, aren't you?"

Before he could say anything, she was walking toward the cabin. Steve pushed his bike into a clump of bushes and dragged branches across the opening to hide it from prying eyes. He stepped back and ran his eye over his work, grunting in satisfaction. He took a walk around the cabin, noting all the entrances, happy to see that all of the windows could be shuttered and locked from the inside, and that the trees had been cleared to provide an open view of the perimeter.

By the time that Steve was satisfied that anyone approaching the cabin would be doing so across open ground, and that if they reached the cabin, they would find it a harder nut to crack than they might have expected, the sun was low on the horizon. When he opened the cabin door, Katherine had already made herself at home and was looking through a cupboard.

"There's enough food in here to last for months."

"Hopefully it won't be needed; this is only meant to be a temporary stop," Steve said. "But, always nice to know that it's there if it comes down to it. There's something even better, though."

"What's that?"

Steve tossed her a towel. "Two bathrooms and plenty of hot water. I don't know about you, but I feel like a long shower after that ride. There's a spring that feeds the tanks, so we won't run out."

"I'm liking your friend more and more," Katherine said. "We could stay here a long time if we needed to."

"It's only a brief stop, I'm afraid. My friend said he would keep out of our hair for the time we need to regroup, but he likes his privacy and doesn't want us here much longer than that."

"At least we'll have a nice view."

"After we freshen up, I think we need to have a talk," Steve said.

"I guess so, but your friend had better have stocked up on coffee."

* * *

Steve placed a steaming cup of coffee in front of Katherine and then took the seat across the kitchen table from her.

"How are you feeling?" he asked her.

She hesitated as if she were going to put on a brave face, and then sighed and took her coffee mug in both hands. She blew into it, and then took a sip.

"To be honest, I feel a bit shaky now that I have time to think about how close we came to getting killed back there."

"They weren't trying to kill you. In fact, they were trying very hard to avoid it."

"I wasn't really talking about them. You and that motor-cycle . . ."

"Very funny. But, it does raise an interesting question—what's changed? From what Maria told me, before, it seemed like they were trying to kill you. Now they're doing everything they can to capture you."

"It's pretty obvious, isn't it?" she asked.

Steve flushed. "Not to me, it isn't."

"Sorry, I didn't mean to make you feel stupid or anything. I keep forgetting that you've just come in on all this. The thing is, all my close calls happened when I was still working at S.H.I.E.L.D. Anyway, even if it was encrypted, all my research was there, stored on site. I didn't keep it with me."

"Let me guess," Steve said. "You deleted everything on your way out the door."

"Exactly!" Katherine said with a smile. "See? You aren't just all big muscles, there's a brain in there."

"Um . . . thank you?"

"So, the difference is now they aren't trying to silence me, they're trying to get their hands on my research."

"That makes sense," Steve said. "But it doesn't make you safe. If they were willing to kill you to keep you quiet and steal your research, then I doubt they'll draw the line at a bit of torture to get it out of you."

"I wish I could say that I thought you were wrong, but that's what I think as well."

Steve simply looked at her for a moment. The more he got to know Katherine, the more he admired her. He knew plenty of people who would have been a blubbering mess in this situation, but the only sign that gave away the tension she must have been feeling was the way she was biting her lower lip. She could have been talking about an interesting software problem, rather than contemplating the existence of people who might kill or torture her given a half a chance.

"Katherine." She looked up from her coffee at the sound of her name. "Don't you think it's time to tell me exactly what this project of yours was?"

For a moment, he thought he had pushed too hard and too quick. A stubborn look in her eyes, she gazed at him coolly for a moment, studying him intently and giving him the uncomfortable feeling of being weighed and measured. If that was what she was doing, the scales must have tilted in his favor.

"I guess I owe you that much. Crazy motorcycle shenanigans aside, you saved my life—or at least saved me from some very unpleasant stuff. You've shown that you've got my best interests at heart, even if we might disagree on exactly what those are." She nodded to herself and began, "How much do you know about computers?"

Steve laughed. "People keep asking me that. Not much. Enough to surf the internet and that sort of thing. About as much about as most drivers know about their cars—how to get it running and take it where they want to go, but not much of what goes on under the hood."

"I'll keep it simple. Just don't get all huffy if it seems condescending—it's only because I'm trying to express something pretty complex in simple terms."

"Trust me, you couldn't possibly be as condescending as the guy who talked me through setting up my phone."

She grinned. "Yeah, we've all been there. What you need to understand is that the internet is the biggest repository of information the world has ever known. That's what makes it so powerful. If you have access to the internet, you have access to information, and information is power. Governments know this, and that's why one of the first things tyrannical governments try to do is limit the information their populace gets. Back in your day, one of the best weapons the Allies had was the radio—Voice of America and the BBC. Using them, they were able to broadcast news to people behind enemy lines who were being kept in the dark about how the war was really going."

Steve nodded. He well remembered listening to those broadcasts, and how the partisans he had fought with had treasured their shortwave radios almost as much as they had their rifles. Whenever they could, they'd tuned in to one of the Allied channels and listened avidly, storing away every scrap of news. During the hardest days of the occupation of

Europe, the Allied broadcasts had been a light shining in the darkness that had helped keep hope alive.

"The internet is like that, times a thousand. Not only can you find out what's happening in the world and share news with millions of other people, you can also read up on history and see what really happened, as opposed to what you've been told. We take it for granted here, but there are a lot of places where that's something radical. When a government's historical narrative is based on lies, there's nothing they fear more than the truth."

Katherine's face had lit up, and her voice was full of passion and excitement. It was obviously a subject that mattered deeply to her.

"That's why so many governments restrict access to the internet. They either filter it, censoring what the big search engines can display, or they block whole swathes of the net completely. The tool that I came up with can circumvent or burrow through anything out there, giving people completely unrestricted access to all of the information that's floating around the web—no matter where they are."

"That's a powerful tool, indeed," Steve said. "Even I know that."

"Right?" Katherine said. "Originally, my idea was that we could use it to help revolutions against tyrannical regimes or people suffering under oppressive governments, the idea being that instead of imposing our processes on people, we give them the tools to free themselves. But when I took it to my immediate superior, he pointed out something I had missed, something that clearly terrified him."

"What was that?" Steve asked, even though he was pretty sure he knew the answer. He wanted to see how far Katherine had pursued the chain of logic.

"He said that it was a double-edged sword. When I asked him what he meant, he asked me once it was out there, what was going to stop our citizens from using it?"

"And how did you answer?"

"How do you think?" she exclaimed. "I asked why it would matter? We live in a democracy—we shouldn't be trying to hide anything from our citizens."

"What did he say to that?" Steve asked.

"He laughed at me—told me I was naive, that your average person on the street wasn't capable of deciding for themselves what to believe."

By this point, Katherine was fairly shaking with anger, and two red spots had appeared on her cheeks.

"I told him that perhaps that wasn't for him to decide," she said.

"In those words?" Steve asked.

As mad as she was, that got her to smile.

"Maybe not exactly those words. But anyway, after I said it, he blew his top. He told me that he was going to write me up. The next day I got called in to see the department head, and my supervisor was with him. And I got read the riot act. I was told that I needed to have a think about my future and that we would be discussing it again at another meeting."

"And that's when you called Maria?"

"Yeah, she did a pretty good job of calming me down and we had a good chat. After my drinks with Aunt Maria, I knew how I had to play it, so when I met with them I told them that they were right—that it was too dangerous, and I would get rid of the research and forget all about it. Played the obedient little drone and all that."

"And were they convinced?" Steve asked.

"Of course. Too convinced. They just about fell over themselves ordering me not to destroy anything, claiming that it might be able to be repurposed. I just nodded and smiled, but I knew that what they meant was that they wanted to find a way of using it against other countries without having to worry about it coming back to bite them."

"They?"

"Oh, not them personally. But careers have been built on far less than that. I'm sure they could see a lot of promotions in their future." She paused for a moment. "Or a lot of money. But there was no way they were getting their hands on it. All they had were schematic files, and there was no way they could re-create my research from that. They needed the originals, but all of our workstations are locked down with our own personal encryption. That way, even if anyone managed to hack into the S.H.I.E.L.D. system, they wouldn't be able to get into individual computers. Of course, that means it's just as safe from internal threats, especially after I disabled the supervisor overrides. I mean, eventually they might have been able to get to it, but it would have taken a lot of time and effort, and I would have known."

"They were so wrong about you, weren't they? You aren't naive at all."

She blushed slightly, and then went on.

"Then the accidents started. The subway. The fire in the rubbish bins behind my apartment building. Lots of little things. And I figured that they either wanted all the credit for themselves, or someone had offered them enough money that it was worth it to make me disappear."

"Or they were worried you would take it to the public."

"Yeah, but I like to think I was pretty convincing when I told them I'd seen the light. I told them that I hadn't really thought through the consequences, thanked them even."

"Sometimes even a slight doubt is too much risk when there's enough money at stake—or enough power."

She shrugged. "Whatever it was, I decided that it was time to make myself scarce. I deleted every trace of my research, except for my personal backups, and then called for help. Aunt Maria and I had arranged a signal, just in case. She might be paranoid, but sometimes that comes in handy."

"And here we are."

"Yep, here we are. So what do you think? What should I have done? Should I have gone public with it?"

Steve considered his words very carefully. He knew that she wasn't going to like what he was about to say.

"A lot of people tell me I'm old fashioned, and they're probably right. I believe in this country, and one of the greatest things about it is the right to freedom of speech." Katherine opened her mouth to say something, but he cut her off. "But I also remember being at war and some of the slogans I used to see. 'Loose lips sink ships' and all that. Maybe sometimes the government does need to keep secrets—when there are lives at stake."

Katherine gave him an incredulous look. "I can't believe what I'm hearing. I expected better than simplistic arguments like that from you."

"Why? I'm just a simple soldier. I'm not a philosopher or a theologian. All I know is that the difference between right and wrong is usually pretty simple. We just like to complicate it, especially when we're trying not to do what doing the right thing dictates." Steve sighed and took another sip of his coffee. "But I don't know what the answer is in all this, or how we find the balance between security and freedom. I leave questions like that to people at higher pay grade. I just want to stop the bad guys."

"And when you leave it to other people, you become complicit in their decisions," Katherine said. "Do you really think it stops with keeping secrets in wartime, or with saving lives? Next it's 'when it's in the national interest,' and that covers a multitude of sins. At least when there are no secrets, you can tell who the bad guys are."

Steve though about that for a moment.

"Look, I need to think about that for a while, okay? We're here for a few days at least, and I promise that I won't make any decisions on your behalf about what to do about it. As far as I'm concerned, my job is keeping you alive, and that's it. For now. Okay?" Katherine didn't say anything and he repeated himself, louder. "Okay?"

She nodded grudgingly.

"I guess I can't ask any more than that. For now."

Chapter 6

APPALACHIAN MOUNTAINS,
NORTH CAROLINA: TIME UNKNOWN

Over the next few days Steve and Katherine took the opportunity to rest up, enjoying life without people shooting at them. To begin with, they spent their time in solitary thought; their earlier discussion had left them both a little cautious of one another, neither one wanting to be the one who sparked another disagreement. The cabin was big enough that there was room for two people to be alone, and they each picked a place that they made their own. For Katherine, it was the swing seat on the cabin's porch, where she would simply sit and look out over the valley, finding a sense of peace in the incredible views. Steve spent most of his time in the den, browsing the extensive library. The room's shelves were groaning under the weight of an eclectic collection of books, and Steve occupied himself with a series of mysteries featuring a hard-bitten idealist who lived on a boat in Florida. The only time that they talked was when they sat down for meals, which each of them took a turn to cook.

By necessity, having often acted as the company cook in the field, Steve had learned how to prepare a number of simple dishes. Katherine wasn't a big fan of cooking, but made far better coffee than the paint-stripper strength brew Steve was used to. It didn't take them long to settle into a comfortable routine, and before the end of the week some of the tension had slowly eased away. They avoided certain subjects, but still found their mealtime conversations lasting longer as they got to know each other. It turned out that they had more in common than Steve would have thought, but it was disconcerting for him to realize that a lot of what had been the latest and greatest to him was fashionably retro to Katherine. Still, it was nice to mention a musician and have someone actually recognize the name, and he tried not to think too much about how many years had passed since the day he had heard that musician for the first time. Katherine did try and introduce him to some newer music, but it turned out that their tastes weren't that in sync.

They were sitting down to dinner on the fourth night— the evening's menu featuring the haute cuisine of baked beans on toast with a side of franks—when the conversation turned to their mutual acquaintance. Steve had been waiting for Katherine to ask, and was surprised it had taken so long.

"So, how did you meet Aunt Maria?" Katherine asked him.

"We've known each other for years. She was Nick's right hand . . . um, woman . . . for a long time, so I was aware of her before we really talked," Steve said. "She used to stand next to him at briefings looking like she'd put a bullet in you if you didn't pay attention."

"That sounds like Aunt Maria," Katherine said, laughing. "I didn't see that much of her growing up, but I was still more scared of her finding out about bad grades than I was of my mom finding out."

"We went on a few operations together, and it didn't take me long to realize she was a good soldier to have at your side . . . or at your back."

"What sort of operations?" Katherine asked curiously.

"You know I can't say. Maybe Maria will tell you sometime if you ask really nicely." Katherine's face communicated quite eloquently what she thought about that, and he went on. "Let's just say that they weren't exactly holidays. Lots of people trying to kill us, and some came pretty close."

"Interesting," Katherine said, and went back to eating. He caught her looking at him during the rest of meal, but she didn't pursue the topic any further. Throughout the next day, he noticed that she seemed to have something on her mind, and that night, as they sat down for dinner again, she raised it again.

"You saved Aunt Maria's life?"

"A couple of times. But no more often than she saved

mine." Steve was quiet for a minute, remembering the sound of bullets whistling through the air and the smell of dirt in his nostrils as he pressed his face into the ground. "It wasn't war in the official sense of the word, you know, but when you've fought together, been under fire together—it doesn't matter where it is—it's a bond you can't explain."

"So, that's why she trusted you?" Katherine asked. "You can trust people you've been through that sort of thing with?"

"No, facing death with someone doesn't magically make them trustworthy. Some of the guys I served with I wouldn't have trusted as far as I could kick them—until the bullets started flying. It just meant that we already had some common ground, and I guess we saw enough of each other in action to build up a healthy professional respect for each other."

"I suppose that makes sense," Katherine said. "She doesn't speak much about her work, but the few times you came up, she spoke highly of you."

"That's nice to hear," Steve said. "I'd hoped she felt that way, but she was never the easiest person to read."

"Unlike me, you mean."

It was a statement, not a question, but she was smiling, so Steve was reasonably certain she was poking fun, and was not actually offended.

"Let's just say I'm never uncertain of what you think about something."

He winked at her, and they laughed, together.

* * *

The next day, Steve woke to the sound of a truck pulling into the driveway. He was out of bed in a heartbeat, and carefully made his way to the front of the house, making sure that at no time was he silhouetted in the windows. Carefully, he peered around the corner of the window and looked out at the yard. He let out a sigh of relief.

"It's okay, Katherine, it's a friend," he yelled. "You can come out."

She stumbled into the room, hair tousled and rubbing her eyes sleepily. She looked at him blankly.

"What? Why couldn't I come out?"

"Never mind. Get dressed, we have company."

"You get dressed! Jeez."

"What? Oh." Steve looked down and blushed, realizing he was still in his boxers. "Sorry!"

"I'm scandalized. That's not way to act in front of an innocent young lady."

She said it with a perfectly straight face, and he was starting to apologize again when she burst out laughing.

"Very funny," he grumbled.

Leaving her to shower, Steve went and threw on his clothes, then hurried out of the house.

"Jeremiah!" he exclaimed. "It's good to see you again."

The older man unfolded himself out of the truck. It was

a battered old pickup with a gun rack in the rear window and a truck bed full of tools and traps—as well as a number of rabbit carcasses. The only thing that distinguished the truck from a thousand others was the complete absence of bumper stickers. Jeremiah himself could have been anywhere from forty to sixty, his nut-brown skin weathered and cracked from long days spent outdoors. He was lean, stringy muscle wrapped around a bony frame that topped Steve by half a foot. He reached out and clasped Steve's hand, his grip speaking of strength held back.

"Good to see you too, son." His voice was raspy and subdued. "Hope the cabin was suitable."

"It was everything we could have asked for," Steve said. "Thank you for letting me use it on such short notice. I owe you."

"Don't insult me with talk of owing. I remember what you did for me."

Steve shrugged. "It was nothing. Just doing what was right."

"It wasn't nothing to me," Jeremiah said.

"Anyway, why don't you come inside?" Steve said changing the subject, embarrassed by all the talk of owing. "There's coffee. Well, you know that; it's yours, anyway, but I mean there's a pot ready if you want some."

"Don't mind if I do."

By the time they got to the kitchen, Katherine had already

served herself a cup of coffee and was sitting at the table. The two men joined her and Steve made the introductions, Katherine and Jeremiah sizing each other up.

"Thank you for the use of your cabin, Mr.—?"

"Tyler, but Jeremiah'll be fine, sweetheart."

"And Katherine will be fine for me, Jeremiah," Katherine said firmly.

Jeremiah laughed. "This one doesn't take any guff from no one, does she, Steve?"

Steve nodded. "Bit like you."

"Well, Katherine," Jeremiah said, emphasizing her name, "It was my pleasure. No matter what he says, I figure I owe Steve big, and this is just a little payment off that debt. Did he tell you what he did for me?"

"No, he's been very reticent about the whole thing," Katherine replied.

"Yeah, he is a bit too modest for his own good."

"I'd love to hear about it," she said.

"Do we have to?" Steve asked plaintively. "Why don't we just drink our coffee?"

Jeremiah ignored him.

"Depending on which side of the family you look at, my family have either been here on this mountain for hundreds of years—or for thousands. I don't really care too much for the outside world; I'm pretty happy just sitting here in my cabin when I'm not out hunting. I grow my own food, and as you can see, water and power ain't a problem as long as the sun shines and the rain falls. I grow plenty of my own food, and what I can't grow for myself, I trade for."

"What do you trade?" Katherine asked.

"All sorts of things. I make furniture, and I even turn my hand to sculpture. I do handyman jobs for people, and sometimes I even have enough meat and skins left over for those don't like to hunt themselves. I keep myself pretty busy, but it's worth it. You've seen the view."

Both of his guests nodded.

"Steve and I got to know each a few years back when I helped him and a few others track down someone. I know this mountain and all its valleys like the back of my hand, and finding a trail wasn't much of a problem for me. When it was all done with, I had myself a brand new rifle, and Steve and I got along well enough given he ain't from around here."

"And the favor?" Katherine prompted.

"I was getting to it. About a year later, I started getting letters from the government, telling me that I owed them this much for that, and that much for this. Seemed like they had decided I needed to pay for the privilege of living on the land what had been in my family ever since there was people around here." He turned to spit on the ground, then remembered he had company. "I just threw the letters away. I'm a law-abiding citizen and I try not to bother the government, but I expect them not to bother me in return. I don't ask for anything from them except to be left alone."

"So what happened?"

"The letters kept coming, and I kept throwing them out, but one day the sheriff showed up with some city man in a suit. He told me unless I paid twenty thousand they were going to take my house, and I couldn't let that happen."

"What did you do?"

"I know some folks, they would have made threats, shot at anyone who came on their land. But I don't hold much with that sort of thing—as I said, I'm a law-abiding man. But I didn't have two thousand in cash, let alone twenty. That's when I remembered Steve here. I gave him a call, and he told me sit tight, so I did." Jeremiah grinned, revealing a perfect set of teeth. "Next thing I knew, I got another visit and was told I didn't have to worry about the money, and never would."

Katherine turned to look at Steve, who shifted uncomfortably.

"How did you manage that?" she asked.

"It was no big deal," Steve said. "I just made a few phone calls, called in a favor or two, and pointed out how much bad press there would be in forcing Jeremiah off his land. It was nothing, really. Jeremiah is making too big a deal about it."

"Nothing?" Katherine exclaimed. "I know what government red tape is like. You must have been really convincing."

Steve shrugged. "I like to think that people will do the right thing if you give them the chance. I just didn't think it was right that someone like Jeremiah should suffer because of bureaucracy. The government is there to help people, not make life harder for them."

"I would have thought that you'd be all for sticking by rules and regulations, whether you agreed with them or not," Katherine said. "You're meant to be the poster child for Uncle Sam, after all."

"The spirit of the law is what's important," Steve said. "Those laws weren't meant to penalize people like Jeremiah. It really wasn't a big deal."

"As I said, it sure was a big deal to me. I really had no idea what I was going to do, and having to leave this place, it would have killed me. I ain't got no children, but my sister's boy will take over when I'm gone—if he wants, I guess. But I didn't want to be the one who broke the chain that stretched all the way back, and Steve here made sure that I wasn't. I can't think of anyone else who would have done that for me. So, when he asked to use the cabin for a few days, it was the least I could do. I figure it doesn't come close to paying him back, but it's a start."

"I don't need to be paid for doing the right thing," Steve said. "But, thank you, Jeremiah. You really came through."

"Do you need more time?" the older man asked. "I won't lie—I like my privacy, but you can stay a little longer if there's a need. I did a check of my traplines while I was giving you some privacy, and I got me more rabbits than I need. I could cook you up some real nice stew."

Steve looked over at Katherine.

"As much as I've enjoyed the break, it's time we got going. We have places to be."

Katherine nodded.

"Yeah, it is tempting to just hole up here and pretend everything is okay, but I'd rather find out what exactly I'm facing. Plus, this guy has terrible taste in music."

"Not wrong there," Jeremiah said. "Well, as long as you're sure, then, we should make our good-byes. Never was one to believe in drawing them out."

Steve had his own thoughts on good-byes, and how having a chance to say any sort of farewell was better than none, but he didn't want to bring the mood down. Instead, he smiled and said good-bye to Jeremiah. Thirty minutes later, Steve and Katherine were on the bike heading back to the city. The noise of the bike would have made it impossible anyway, but neither were in the mood for talking. Steve was filled with a sense of foreboding—taking Katherine back into danger went against every instinct he possessed. He could only trust that Maria had a plan.

By the time they descended from the hills, it was dark and the lights of the city were spread out before them, pointing into the city's heart like a spear of asphalt. The ride back had been as unpleasant as the one out of the city had been, and Katherine had some choice words to say when she saw the apartment they were to hide out in.

The super had been happy to take cash in exchange for one of the empty rooms in the run-down building, and hadn't asked their names. His knowing smirk at the sight of the older man with his obviously younger companion had set Steve's teeth on edge, but he had consoled himself with the thought that it was a common scenario that wouldn't stick in the man's memory. Not wanting to spend a moment longer in the lobby than necessary, Steve hadn't been willing to wait for the elderly elevator to descend, and had insisted that they take the stairs. Remembering the man's smirk had kept Rogers grumpy all the way up the seemingly endless flights of stairs, and he barely responded to Katherine's teasing. She had thought the super's assumption hilarious, and had plenty to say, except toward the end of the climb when she was saving her breath for the next flight of stairs. Steve wasn't breathing heavily in the slightest; he could have run up and down the staircase without breaking a sweat. But he took the high ground, and didn't point that out to Katherine.

The apartment was on the tenth floor, and the three small rooms were dim and shabby, with a smell of mildew and neglect that gave the air an unpleasant tang. When they had opened the door, something had scuttled back into the hole from whence it had come, and Katherine made a small, choked sound of disgust.

"You've got to be kidding," Katherine exclaimed. "I wouldn't keep my pets in here."

"It's like a palace compared to the one I grew up in," Steve said mildly. "Brooklyn was very different when I was kid. Now I can't even afford a place there."

"You sound like my dad."

"Well, technically I'm old enough to be your grandfather," Steve said, hoping for a smile. When he didn't get one, he went on. "Look, we'll only be here a few days."

"I suppose I can survive," Katherine said. "So, what are we going to do while we wait?"

"I'm going to do a bit of looking around. In every city there's always a place, or more than one, where a certain type of people go to find work," Rogers said. "They're clearing houses for information, and there's always someone there who knows who's paying, and for what."

"I thought Aunt Maria was doing the investigating," Katherine said accusingly. "Shouldn't we wait for word from her?"

"I've already spoken to her," Steve said. "Just before we left. She's been very busy, and she's set up a meeting for me with someone who has some information for me."

"And you didn't tell me this before, why?" Katherine demanded. "And why didn't you let me talk to her?"

"We can't risk long phone calls—the less contact we have with her, the safer it is," Steve said. "Besides, she didn't give me a chance to say much, just asked for a quick status report, gave me the information I needed, and hung up. It wasn't exactly a social call."

"You still could have told me," she muttered.

"I didn't tell you because I knew you'd be mad about it. I didn't relish the thought of you spending the whole trip sulking."

"I don't sulk," Katherine said. "You should have told me. This is my life at stake."

Steve had to admit she had a point.

"You're right," he said. "I'm sorry."

Katherine looked at him in surprise.

"You mean that?"

"Yes, you have a right to know these things," Steve said. "When I get back tonight I'll fill you in on everything I know so far."

"Um, surely you know I'm coming with you, right?"

"What?" Steve said. "That's not the way it works."

"If you go without me, I won't be here when you get back."

"You really would be better off here," Steve said. "You think this place is a dump? Wait until you get a load of where I'm going. It's a disgusting place full of disgusting people."

"Sounds like the clubs my friends drag me to sometimes,"

Katherine said. "Steve, stop treating me like a fragile flower—I'm not half as delicate as you seem to think I am."

"I know—it's just, old habits die hard," Steve said. "I was raised to treat a lady—I mean a woman, sorry—a certain way. It's hard to overcome that sort of upbringing, even if I wanted to."

"Well, you don't need to change too much, Steve. If you weren't so straitlaced you wouldn't be you anymore," she said with what sounded affection in her voice. "Just don't make the mistake of thinking I'm fragile. This affects me, and I don't want you keeping me out of helping find out what we need to know out of some paternalistic concern."

Steve sighed. He was smart enough to know when he was fighting a losing battle, and decided not to prolong the inevitable.

"I'll do my best, but at the risk of sounding like a parent—let's get some sleep. We have a big day ahead of us tomorrow."

Chapter 7

A hush fell across the room as Steve and Katherine stepped into the bar, and it felt like every eye in the barroom was staring at them. After a few seconds that seemed to stretch out forever, the conversations started up again as the patrons turned back to whatever business they were conducting.

"You take me to such nice places," Katherine said sardonically, looking around.

Steve had to agree; it wasn't the nicest bar he'd ever been in, and he'd seen some pretty rank dives in his time. The place reeked of cigarette smoke and vomit, and there were stains on the carpet that could have been anything from beer to blood, and that were probably a mix of both. The fittings were beaten and battered, and the beer looked weak and watered down. Anyone walking in off the street could have been forgiven for thinking the bar was a low-class establishment for washed-out characters. But a more observant eye would have noticed that most of the patrons were especially well muscled, and that all moved with the air of those accustomed to taking care of themselves. Very few customers were actually doing much drinking, and instead nursed a single drink while they talked. And the eyes, while no longer obviously on the newcomers, were still sizing them up with a sharpness that no drunk possessed.

"You did insist on coming along," Steve said.

"I wasn't staying at the apartment alone," she replied. "Anyway, nothing at this place could compare to the cockroaches in that dump you found for us."

Steve didn't have much faith in his hasty disguise of a trench coat and sunglasses, but it had been the best he could do. Even if his face hadn't been on the news again and again, he had encountered many of the people currently sizing him up, so he figured it was only a matter of time before someone recognized him. The crowd was a mix of low-level villains and criminals. Some were experienced mercenaries, while others had minor powers of their own that they now applied to petty crime—they were the kind of people who made a living working for those with real power and money. It wasn't that they weren't good at what they did, or dangerous in their own way—it was simply that they didn't play in the big leagues. These were the people that Steve went through to get to the really bad guys. These people would escape in the chaos, or get picked up and do a little time, and then they'd get hired by the next megalomaniac bent on world domination.

That didn't mean the people in the bar could be taken for granted. Steve stayed alert and ready as he moved through the room, knowing that many of these people would bear grudges for the times that they had come up against him and paid the price. If someone did recognize him, he could only hope that those encounters were still fresh enough in their minds that they would be dissuaded from trying anything now. The bar was known as a no-combat zone, a place where criminals could conduct their business without worrying about too much attention from the authorities, and so they refrained from doing anything ostentatious that might attract notice. But custom only stretched so far—it would only take one person letting his need for vengeance get the better of him to set off a mob.

As Steve and Katherine neared the bar, the bartender looked up from listlessly swabbing at a ground-in stain with a dirty rag. He had a pale, sallow face, a pencil-thin mustache, and lank, greasy black hair that was combed away from a ruler-straight side part.

"What can I getcha?"

"I'm looking for a man called Wóbser," Steve said.

"Sorry, don't know him. Bar is for paying customers only, friend, so what can I getcha? Or do I need to ask you to leave?"

Steve sighed, and pulled out a hundred-dollar bill. He placed it in front of the bartender, who reached for it. Before it could disappear, Steve's hand flashed out as quick as a snake and grabbed the man's wrist. Steve squeezed, not hard enough to cause any damage, but hard enough to let the man know that he could if he wanted to.

"Are you sure you don't know my friend . . . friend?" Steve asked.

"Now that I think about it, I think I do," the man said weakly. "He's over there, in the corner booth."

Steve looked over to where the bartender pointed at a big blond man sitting with his friends, laughing at some joke. The smile didn't reach the man's green eyes, which were as cold and appraising as a reptile's. He was dressed in a blue business suit, but it was straight off the rack, not a tailored item, so when Wóbser twisted a certain way in his seat, Steve could make out the bulge of a gun in a shoulder holster. The two men next to Wóbser didn't look like much to worry about; they had the look of sycophants trying to ride Wóbser's coattails. They'd follow his lead, for good or bad, but at the sign of any real trouble Steve had no doubt they'd skulk away like rats deserting a sinking ship.

"Thank you. That's very helpful of you," Steve said. He released the bartender's wrist and grimaced as he wiped his hand on his trouser leg, not liking the oily feel of the man's skin.

Rogers was halfway across the room when he realized that Katherine was no longer with him. He looked back to find that she had been stopped in her tracks by a huge figure looming over her. Steve moved quickly toward them, but before he could reach them, the man reached out and grabbed Katherine's upper arm. He was almost seven feet tall, with a sloping brow and thick, black, curly hair. Steve recognized him from S.H.I.E.L.D.'s files—he was a low-level metahuman called Sergi who made a living as hired muscle. He didn't have super strength—just that proportionate to that weight of muscle—but given that he must have weighed about three hundred and fifty pounds and none of it fat, that was normally enough power to deal with most normal threats to his employer of the day. Next to Sergi, Katherine looked childlike, resembling a doll that he could snap like a twig if he chose.

That didn't seem to bother Katherine at all and, as Steve watched, she drove her fist into the big man's stomach. Sergi barely flinched, but Katherine shook her hand in pain. It didn't faze her for long, though, and Sergi's booming laugh was cut off as she brought her knee up into his groin, doubling him over. When he straightened, all the humor had left his brutal face, and real anger clouded his expression. But by then, Steve was there and as Sergi swung a fist the size of a brick, Rogers reached up and caught it in his hand. Sergi's look of surprise changed to one of pain as Steve squeezed and bones creaked.

"People tell me I'm old fashioned," Steve said evenly. "It's probably true. I might even be boring, I don't know. But one thing I do know is that bothering young ladies who obviously don't want to bothered is not very gentlemanly. Wouldn't you agree?"

"Stick it up your—"

Steve squeezed harder and Sergi sank to his knees with a moan. Such was his size that even on his knees he was looking straight into Steve's eyes. Steve stared back at him.

"I said, wouldn't you agree?"

Steve squeezed again, and this time he heard something pop.

"Yes, yes!" Sergi gasped. "It's not very gentlemanly!"

"I guess you have something to say to the lady?"

"Um, I'm sorry?" Sergi ground the apology out between gritted teeth.

"That's better," Steve said. He turned his head slightly to look at Katherine. "Do you accept his apology?"

Katherine was trying not to laugh. "Sure."

"Then let that be the end of it."

He released Sergi's hand, leaving the bigger man still on his knees and nursing his battered fist. He and Katherine were walking toward Wóbser when Steve heard a whisper of noise behind him. He spun just in time to catch Sergi's massive fist right on the point of his chin. The sheer momentum behind it sent Rogers flying, landing on his back. Sergi loomed over him, raising a huge boot-clad foot over the prostrate hero, but before he could bring it down on Steve's head, Katherine drove her foot into the back of Sergi's knee with all her power. The joint bent around the blow, and Sergi let out a bellow of pain as he fell to one knee. Before he could stand up, Katherine pivoted into a perfect roundhouse kick, burying the ball of her foot in Sergi's solar plexus.

Even as all the air left his lungs with an explosive grunt and he hunched forward around the blow, Katherine was grabbing Sergi's hair and bringing her knee up to meet his face. Even after a second blow he wouldn't go down, and still swayed slightly, but Katherine wasn't finished. She balled both of her hands into one fist, and wound up, her hands finishing almost behind her head. She brought her fist through in a whistling arc, using all the power her body could generate, and hit Sergi on the back of his neck. There was crunch, and Sergi toppled forward with a crash that rattled the bottles on the mirrored shelves behind the bar.

The whole exchange had lasted perhaps fifteen seconds, if that, and was over by time Steve regained his feet. He walked over to the unconscious figure and, none to gently, poked him with his toe. Sergi didn't even flinch, and certainly didn't look like he would be getting up again. Steve flipped him over onto his back and checked his airways, then turned back to Katherine, who was waiting for him.

"You're right, you know," she said.

"What do you mean?"

"You really are old fashioned. It's not necessarily a bad thing, as long as you don't make the mistake of thinking I can't look after myself."

Despite the ache in his chin, Steve couldn't help but laugh. "Oh, I would never do that."

Wóbser was now alone in his booth, his companions either dismissed by him or having decided that discretion was the better part of valor. He looked up at his two visitors, and gestured for them to take a seat.

"Mr. Rogers. Or do you prefer Captain America?"

"Steve is fine. You know who I am?"

Wóbser laughed. "Do I look blind? You are all over the television, and even if I hadn't seen that, the example you made of Sergi would have made it clear you weren't just someone in off the street. Don't worry, part of my service is discretion, or I wouldn't get any repeat customers. Your secrets are safe with me."

He turned his smile to Steve's companion. "And this must be Katherine. Very formidable indeed."

Steve made a mental note. Wóbser liked the sound of his own voice, and he liked showing off his knowledge. It might just be an attempt to establish his bona fides, but Steve thought it more likely that he just liked impressing people. He'd dealt with Wóbser's type before, many times, and that desire to impress could be used against him. Act suitably awed, and they would often be so gratified that they'd let more slip than they intended to.

"I guess you already know why we're here, right?" Steve asked.

Wóbser shaped his hand into the shape of a gun and pointed it at Katherine.

"You want to know how much she is worth. And who is after her."

"That's right. Maybe you do know everything that's worth knowing in this city."

"What's in it for me, though? That's the question here."

"I'd been told that you've already been paid for this information," Rogers said. "Our mutual friend would be very displeased if she heard you'd tried to renege on that deal—and you really don't want to make her unhappy. Trust me on that."

"Perhaps she should have warned me exactly how much interest there is in the girl, and the players involved. The information she wanted is worth twice what I've been paid—and I can't spend it if I am dead."

"I'd owe you a favor. How does that sound?"

"A favor from Captain America," Wóbser said musingly. "That's a valuable commodity right there."

"You know the sort of things you can ask of me, and what I won't do. No breaking the law, no hurting innocent people.

The obvious. But if you ever need help, I will do whatever I can for you."

"And how do I know that when I call on this favor you will come through for me? Maybe you'll forget what you promised."

Steve leaned forward, muscles flexing under his jacket as he cracked his knuckles. "Are you implying I would break my word?"

For the first time the smug look on Wóbser's face slipped, and a bead of sweat appeared on his left temple.

"No, no! Of course not," he said hurriedly. "Your word is good with me."

Steve sat back and relaxed, smiling as Wóbser took out a monogrammed silk handkerchief and dabbed at his brow.

"Glad to hear it. So, what can you tell us?"

"Your friend here is almost as valuable as your word." The smug look was back on Wóbser's face as he looked Katherine up and down. "Two million dollars for her, alive and unhurt. As you can imagine, that's attracted a lot of attention."

Katherine had a slightly stunned look on her face.

"Two million. Wow." She laughed, a little too loudly. "Well, it's nice to be wanted, I guess."

Steve looked around, wondering who was listening to the conversation. That was a lot of money; people were killed every day for a fraction of that amount.

"Of course," Wóbser said. "It doesn't seem quite as much

given who she seems to have picked up as a bodyguard. That will discourage a lot of the minor players. It's not just you that they'd be worried about, either. The company you keep can be . . . intimidating."

"And who is financing such a generous sum, Wóbser?" Steve asked.

"Does the name Jonah Beckham ring a bell?"

Steve thought for a moment, searching for a phantom memory. The name rang a bell, but why? Then he remembered the attacker in the safe house, with the twin staves. He had known that voice, after all.

"Jonah Beckham, you said?" Steve asked. Wóbser nodded, and Steve went on. "When I last ran into him he was a S.H.I.E.L.D. operative. One of their best field agents, though I didn't always approve of his methods. He was an 'ends justify the means' sort of guy. Why would he be trying to capture her?"

"Hey, I'm sitting right here," Katherine said. "Maybe try asking me?"

Steve sighed, and turned to her.

"I'm sorry, Katherine. What do you think?"

"That's better. Jonah Beckham hasn't worked at S.H.I.E.L.D. for almost a year now. He got a transfer to another agency." She thought for a moment. "I don't think anyone ever said which one. But the way people were talking, it was a move up for him."

"He could be working for anyone." Steve stopped when he saw how attentively Wóbser was listening. "We can discuss this later."

He turned back to Wóbser.

"Anything else you can tell us?"

"There's more than one person looking for your girl."

"I'm not anyone's girl."

Wóbser shrugged. "Whatever. But there is some serious muscle. The kind of heavy hitters that might think two million is more than enough to tangle with the Star Spangled Hammer over here. Sergi is minor league in comparison."

"Star Spangled Hammer?" Katherine snickered. "Ha, good one."

"Can you give me any names?" Steve asked, ignoring her. "It would help if I knew who I might be dealing with."

"Sorry, I can't. And before you say it, I am not holding out more for more favors," Wóbser said. "Some of those people, I don't know whether even you could protect me if word got out. Anyway, I have a reputation to protect, too."

Steve suspected that it was more the former concern than the latter that weighed heavier on Wóbser's mind, but he refrained from saying so. Everyone had their pride, after all.

He stood up and pulled out Katherine's chair as she got to her feet.

"Thank you for your help, Wóbser. I won't forget it."

The outside air was a welcome relief after the closed-in

atmosphere of the bar, and Steve breathed in a chest full of clean, fresh air. He felt vaguely unclean, and he had a sudden urge to have a long, hot shower and scrub himself with soap.

"Aunt Maria has some interesting friends," Katherine said.

"They aren't her friends, just people we have to deal with from time to time," Steve said. "She's probably never even met Wóbser, but we deal people like that all the time. I know I've had to sit down across from a hundred guys like him over the years, trying to get information from them about even more guys. It's one of the unfortunate realities of this job; one that I hate."

"Hate?" Katherine asked. "What do you mean?"

"I don't like dealing with men like that, or the other people you find in a place like this. The only thing they respect is strength, so I have to throw my weight around," Steve said. "The thing I've always hated most is a bully. People who push around those who are weaker than themselves." He looked down at himself. "You know, I wasn't always like this, right?"

Katherine nodded. "I've heard rumors. Some sort of super-soldier experiment, right?"

"I was the original ninety-seven-pound weakling—like the guy in the ad who gets sand kicked in his face. Do they still have those?"

Katherine shook her head and Steve laughed.

"Yeah, somehow I didn't think so. What sort of world are we living in?"

"You're just old," she teased. "But don't worry, I know the ones you mean. More from send-ups of them on cartoons than from anything else."

"They turned me down when I tried to enlist, you know? It was one of the worst days of my life." Steve looked up at the sky, remembering what had happened next. "Then they changed me, and all of a sudden I was stronger and faster than any of the bullies who used to push me around. But I didn't want revenge on them."

"What did you want?" Katherine asked softly.

"The same thing I had always wanted. I just wanted to serve my country, and protect those who couldn't protect themselves. I know what it is to be powerless, and I've always tried to stand up for those who can't stand up for themselves. The only difference was now I had the ability to do that—but just because I'd changed on the outside didn't mean I'd changed on the inside." He shrugged. "That's what I signed up to fight for, just on a bigger scale. The Germans, the Japanese, what were they if not bullies? They thought that because they were strong, they could oppress the weaker nations around them."

Katherine took his hand and squeezed it.

"Steve, you're not a bully. I mean, you can be a real pain, but you aren't a bully. Far from it." She smiled up at him.

"That's something you don't have to worry about."

Steve felt a wave of affection rise up as he smiled back, along with a fierce sense of protectiveness. It was nothing romantic, more like something he imagined you'd feel for a little sister, but he knew that this had gone from being a favor for Maria to being something more. He was personally invested now, and he would see it through to the end, no matter what the price.

Chapter 8

They spent the trip back to their apartment digesting the information that Wóbser had given them. Steve was happy to just let the hum of the motorcycle drown out any possibility of conversation as he ran through plans in his mind. When they arrived, he insisted on checking the apartment first for any signs of intrusion, and it was only when he was sure that the coast was clear that he allowed Katherine in.

They were arguing before they even sat down.

"I don't see what choice we have, Katherine," Steve said. "We need to get you some place safe. By now, Maria should have some idea of who she can trust. I need to contact her and she'll work out a place for you to hole up in while she chases down this Beckham guy."

"Are you insane?" Katherine was nearly screaming. "We can't trust anyone at S.H.I.E.L.D., and with $2 million on my head, I don't think we can trust many people outside of it."

"Then what do you suggest? I'm listening."

"We need to find some people who don't care about the money," Katherine said.

"Good luck with that," Steve muttered.

"I heard that. Now who's the cynic?"

"Two million dollars is a lot of money, Katherine. That would tempt a lot of people, that's all I'm saying."

"I know. Look, I have an idea. There's a group that I've been corresponding with for a long time now. We agree on a lot of things when it comes to freedom of information and the way that the internet should be regulated, but I never joined. Sometimes they're a bit . . . extreme for my tastes. They've done all sorts of crazy stuff, like bombing the electoral office of a senator who was trying to sponsor a bill that would have brought in censorship laws that China would have flinched at." At the look on Steve's face she hurriedly added, "They made sure that the place was empty, and it was at two o'clock in the morning."

"So they're domestic terrorists?" Steve said, frowning.

"Steve, they've never hurt anyone! And, they've gone to great lengths to avoid it happening by mistake. Otherwise, I would never have anything to do with them. Surely you know that?"

Steve nodded reluctantly.

"They don't know the exact nature of my research, but they know it relates to internet freedom. And that's something that they care about. A lot," Katherine said. "I know it might seem strange to you, but to them, it's a cause worth fighting for. They feel the same way about it that some people feel about religion . . . or money."

"I know the type. Fought with and against them. If they think that what you have will advance their cause, then they'll hide you no matter how much money is at stake," Steve said. "It's a possibility, I suppose."

"Come on, Steve. We can hole up with them as long as we want, and you can let Aunt Maria know what we've found out. When she's dealt with the corruption on the inside, she can let us know, but this way there's no chance of us being compromised," Katherine said. "So what do you say? Does it sound like a good plan?"

Steve hesitated, but only for a moment. He was opening his mouth to reply when the crash of shattering glass cut him off. In the blink of an eye, he was between the window and Katherine, his shield reflexively grabbed from where it had been resting and in front of them both quickly enough to block the jagged rain of glass, stopping the deadly shower from slashing their flesh to ribbons.

"I knew that you'd be quick enough. But thank you for protecting her, she's worth a lot to me." The voice paused. "Two million dollars, to be exact."

The intruder was about Steve's height and build, and clad in a white cloak with a hood that shadowed his face.

In his right hand he held a sword about the size and shape of a Roman gladius and, most unsettling of all, in his left was a blue shield that was almost a perfect replica of Steve's. The only difference was that in the center was a red, three pronged symbol that resembled a large, uppercase *T*, its slightly curved arms and straight base reaching out to the rim. Steve knew who the man was—Rogers had heard stories from colleagues and friends who had faced him. He was Taskmaster—mercenary, gun for hire, bounty hunter.

"You really shouldn't count your money before you've earned it," Steve said. "You may have some difficulty in collecting on this one."

"I don't have any concerns about collecting."

Steve flicked his wrist and an extendable baton snapped out from his sleeve. It was about the same length as Taskmaster's sword, and had a reassuring heft in his hand. He grabbed Katherine, and, ignoring her protests, pushed her behind him.

"Stay there," he said. "I mean it. I can't be worrying about you while I'm fighting."

She nodded, and Steve moved into a fighting crouch, waiting for the intruder to make the first move. Taskmaster was fast, moving like quicksilver as he brought his sword flashing through the air. It rang off Steve's shield with a squeal of metal, then was back in position quickly enough to catch Steve's baton on its cross guard. Rogers spun, bringing his shield around in a horizontal arc only for it to be halted, quivering, against the other man's shield. Taskmaster's shield may not have been Vibranium, but it was some sort of alloy that was almost as strong.

They exchanged blows, Steve using his baton like a sword. His baton was made of a titanium alloy that was impossible to damage with anything less than an industrial diamond, but it was soon covered in scratches and notches. As they continued to fight, Steve noticed there was something about the man's fighting style that was very familiar, as if he had faced him before. Then it came to him—the intruder's technique was the spitting image of the Swordsman's, one of the heroes who had fought alongside the Avengers in years past. It was uncanny, perfect even down to the little flourish when Taskmaster returned to his guard position. So striking was the resemblance, that for one crazy moment Steve wondered whether it was in fact the Swordsman, gone rogue and in disguise as a known villain.

Then, with a jolt, it came to him, and Steve remembered Taskmaster's unique gift. In an interrogation video Steve had come across in the S.H.I.E.L.D archives—from one of the few times the man had been captured—Taskmaster had claimed that he had been born with what he called photographic reflexes, which provided him with a specialized form of total recall, an eidetic memory link. All he needed was to watch another fighter and Taskmaster could imitate their style down to the last movement. A lifetime dedicated to honing this gift and training his body for battle had created one of the world's most formidable fighters, matching a body at peak physical fitness and strength with an encyclopedic knowledge of combat. At some point along the way, Taskmaster must have fought the Swordsman and picked up his style. Steve had never been much of a fencer, and it was only his own preternatural reflexes that gave him any chance at all against Taskmaster. He knew he couldn't keep the fight up forever, though, as only an urgent leap back saved him from a slashing cut. An inch closer, and it would have disemboweled him although, as it was, it left him with a shallow gash along his ridged, muscular belly.

Desperately, Steve closed in on Taskmaster and jammed his shield down hard on the other man's blade, right near the hilt. The sudden shock jarred the sword loose from the other man's grip and it clattered to the ground. Before Taskmaster could retrieve the sword, Steve kicked it across the floor where it jammed deep into a skirting board. Rogers took advantage of the intruder's distraction to land a punch in the man's short ribs, his fist sinking deep into muscle. The other man let out a grunt of pain, but retaliated with a brutal strike that left Rogers spitting blood. They traded blows for a few minutes—nothing elegant, just straight boxing. Steve had thought he had some talent with the gloves—one of his favorite workouts in his Army days had been a few rounds with the regimental champion—but the other man's style mixed the speed of Ali, the power of Foreman, and the sheer brutality of Tyson.

Breathily heavily, Steve broke a clinch and retreated toward Katherine. He dropped into a kung fu stance, then launched himself into a series of kicks and punches. Taskmaster blocked each strike, but gradually gave ground. Steve had trained with some of the finest martial arts masters on the planet, and he had combined each of their lessons into a style that suited his augmented body and that had turned him into one of the world's greatest combatants in the process. But Taskmaster had fought many of Steve's teachers, and soon deciphered the pattern of Steve's attack, surging forward with a counterattack of his own. Among the storm of blows, Steve glimpsed snatches of techniques he recognized. That strike to the kidneys was something he'd seen Elektra use to great effect, while that grapple that sent pain shooting up his arm from the elbow lock was vintage Iron Fist. But just because he could recognize the techniques didn't mean he could stop all of them, and more and more of Taskmaster's attacks got through.

Steve broke away again, ripping free from a choke hold through sheer brute strength, and took a brief second to catch his breath. His chest was heaving and he could feel blood trickling down the side of his face from where a nasty kick had split the skin over his eye. Taskmaster was not unscathed—one eye was already blackening enough for it to be noticeable even in the shadows of his hood—and he watched Rogers warily as they circled each other once more. Steve closed in on the other man, trying to dredge up the most obscure fighting techniques he knew, hoping that he could find something that Taskmaster had never seen. He worked his way through a dozen disciplines, from taekwondo to sambo wrestling, but each time, Taskmaster met the challenge and threw it back at Steve.

Trying to distract him, Steve started talking.

"So, who's paying you, Taskmaster, and how much?"

"That's none of your concern, Rogers. You won't be around to see it, anyway."

"We'll see about that, I guess. But maybe we don't have to do it this way. I do have some very rich friends—maybe we can match it."

"As if I believe you would pay me to go away. Even if you could, I have accepted the contract, and once I have done that, I never go back on my word."

Steve had to respect that. Besides, he had only been trying to get information from the bounty hunter; he now knew Taskmaster didn't compromise and would never pay someone off. Wearily, he put his hands up again and clenched his fists.

"Okay, bring it on, then."

Both of the combatants were at the very peak of physical condition, with strength and stamina beyond other men, but the brutal nature of the fight was taking its toll on them both. Taskmaster staggered slightly as he approached Rogers, and the fists at the end of Steve's outstretched arms trembled with the fatigue that wracked his body. Their blows were still full of venom, but they had lost some of their crisp precision, and the fight degenerated into a slugfest. No more fancy footwork, just two men exchanging blows that rocked each other back on their heels, blood and sweat flying at every impact. They were lost in their own private hell, the world around them contracted to the end of a fist and the small area of flesh on which said fist landed.

They were so distracted that neither noticed Katherine until the baton she swung intersected with the back of Taskmaster's head. Steve could see the other man's eyes roll back in their sockets until only the whites showed, then he crumpled to the floor. Steve swayed, and would have fallen if Katherine hadn't rushed to his side and grabbed his arm to steady him. He tried to speak, coughed, and spat a wad of bloody phlegm onto the floor.

"Sorry about that," he said weakly. "Not very polite."

"Steve, are you okay?"

He smiled at her with bloodstained teeth.

"Just bully." He swayed again, and Katherine braced herself. "Didn't I tell you not to move?"

She shrugged. "You looked like you needed some help. Are you complaining?"

He shook his head and winced as pain shot through his head and neck.

"We need to get you to a doctor," she said. "I've never seen anyone take a beating like that, not even in a movie. You're bleeding in a dozen places."

"No!" Steve relaxed his grip on Katherine's arm when he noticed her wince. "I'm sorry. But no doctor. We don't know who might be watching us. We need to get to your friends, or whatever they are."

"Don't try and play the tough guy, Steve." Steve was surprised by the anger in her voice. "You can barely stand up straight, and who knows what internal damage you might have."

Steve was touched by her concern, but they were running out of time. Taskmaster might regain consciousness at any moment and Steve wasn't overly excited at the thought of fighting the man again. Even worse, Taskmaster might have arranged backup and they could get another visitor popping into say "hello." In his current state, Steve wasn't sure that he could provide any sort of obstacle to anyone wanting to do Katherine harm. They needed to get somewhere safe and secluded to give him a chance to heal, and he didn't know many options.

"Honestly, I'll be okay. I heal faster than normal—it's part of what the serum did to me. All I need is some rest, lots of food, and a week or so, and I'll be as good as new."

She looked skeptical.

"Are you sure? I really think you need a doctor."

"Katherine, I've been shot and beaten and frozen. Stabbed, too. Oh, and someone tried to garrote me once. I know how much punishment I can take, and I wouldn't let something silly like pride stop me from getting help if I needed it. But I know my body, and I promise you that this is not as bad as it looks. I won't lie, it hurts—a lot. But I've had worse."

He didn't tell her that he hadn't had much worse, that the Taskmaster had given him the sort of beating he had almost forgotten existed. All that would do was worry her, and that was the last thing that they needed.

"All right, then," Katherine said. "But you have to promise me that if you feel like things are getting worse that you'll let me find a doctor. Deal?"

"Scout's honor," Steve said, holding up his right hand. He immediately regretted the gesture when the movement sent a sharp pain lancing through his ribs. It felt like there was something at least fractured in there, if not completely broken.

"Steve, are you sure you're okay? You just went white as a sheet."

"I'm fine, really," Steve replied. "Now, how do we get in touch with these friends of yours?"

"They aren't my friends," Katherine said automatically,

but she was already tapping away on her phone. "It's pretty simple—using a secure chat app, I leave an encrypted message on a forum hosted on a server in Eastern Europe where it's much harder to trace. It's encrypted with my own PGP key, and there are some code phrases that tell the group where to find me and stuff like that. It will take me about forty-five seconds to send the message, which is not long enough for anyone to triangulate my phone's signal and get a fix on us."

"Okay, I understood about three words of that, but if I got that right, you have a way of letting your friends know where to find us and no one else should be able to work it out?"

"Exactly. You're getting the hang of this," Katherine said.

Her smile was obviously forced, and he could see the panic trying to force its way up and through it. He grabbed her hand.

"Katherine, it's all going to be okay. I promise. Now, let's get out of here."

Slowly, leaning on Katherine for support, Steve staggered out of the apartment, almost collapsing as they walked into the empty hallway. He slumped against the wall of the elevator as they descended, trying not to let on how close he was to falling over. The lobby was deserted, and they made their way onto the street. Lightheadedness washed over Steve and he stumbled, grabbing a lamppost just in time to stop himself from falling face first onto the pavement.

"Steve. Steve." Katherine shook him, concern on her face. "Stay with me, please!"

Her phone chimed and she snatched it. The light of the screen illuminated the look of relief that bloomed on her face.

"Steve, we only have to make it to the corner." She grabbed him under the arm and pulled him upright. "You can do it, I know it."

Steve was so weak that he could barely think or even remember where he was. All he knew was that he was meant to be protecting the young woman who was moving in and out of focus, and that he couldn't let her down. He summoned what strength he had left, and followed her. He had no idea how long they stood at the corner before the van pulled up. It felt like hours, but it could have been mere minutes.

The vehicle itself was nothing out of the ordinary—a battered white panel van that would have looked at home on any building site or in any mall parking lot in the country. It sat idling at the curb for a moment, and then the side door slid open. Three men in ski masks carrying stubby semiautomatics jumped out, covering Steve and Katherine with their weapons.

"What's the code word?" one barked at Steve and Katherine.

"Hey, calm down! What's all this?" Katherine protested. "I thought you were a peaceful protest movement."

All three of the guns were pointed at Katherine now, and Steve tensed, hoping he would be strong enough to take whatever opportunity might present itself.

"The code word," the man yelled. "Now!"

"Okay, okay," Katherine said. "It's panopticon."

After a moment's silence, the three men visibly relaxed, guns dropping to point at the ground.

"Sorry things have gotten out of control," the first man said. "We can't be too careful." He turned to the other two. "Get them into the van."

A pair of strong hands grabbed Steve and he felt himself being lifted into the van. Then everything went black and he knew nothing more.

Chapter 9

Steve woke in a strange bed in a strange room. He turned his head to the side and saw no other furniture and no carpets—just bare floorboards and a door reinforced with metal bars. It was an improvement on his last lodgings in one significant way—it was spotlessly clean, almost sterile—but that was small consolation. Then he saw the stand holding the IV drip that was inserted in his arm. He slowly and gently pulled the needle from his vein, ignoring the slight stab of pain, and let the tube fall to the ground.

At least he wasn't restrained—that was something—and he tried to sit up. The pain was bad, very bad, and he blacked out for a moment. When he came to, he had no idea how much time might have passed. He was much more cautious this time. Slowly, he lifted one leg out of the bed and placed his foot on the floor, and then followed with the other. Grabbing the bedhead, he eased himself to his feet and stood for a moment, heart hammering in his chest and sweat pouring from his brow. He gripped the cold metal of the bed frame with the desperation of a drowning man, knowing that if he fell, he wouldn't be getting up for a long time—at least not under his own power.

It had been a long time since he had felt this battered. Taskmaster had really done a number on him. He knew that he would heal in a few days, a week at most, but in the meantime, every part of his body ached. Once the light-headedness passed, he made his slow, shuffling way to the door. The bars were three-inch steel, but it may as well have been ten or twelve inches for all the chance he had of getting through them. At full strength he might have been able to bend them, or rock them back and forth enough to fatigue the metal and eventually snap it, but he was a long way off being able to do that. He made his painful way back to the bed and lay down again. There was no point wearing himself out or injuring himself further by yelling or hammering on the door. Someone would come eventually, and he would deal with the situation as it arose, but until then, he would take whatever rest he could. He was an old enough soldier to know that a little bit of strength might be the difference if it came down to it.

Sometime later, the sound of bars clicking back and the squeal of badly maintained hinges snapped him from slumber to full alertness in a split second. He took his time sitting up, though, not wanting to give away how badly he was hurt. There were two men—one in a doctor's white coat, the other still in a ski mask and holding a submachine gun that had the distinctive blocky look of a Micro Uzi, or its knock off. The doctor was slender but moved with an awareness of his body that only exceptionally good athletes possessed. He had ginger hair that was swept back from his temples, almost reaching his collar, and wore tastefully rimmed glasses.

The armed man possessed an aura of quiet competence. He made no unnecessary movements, and constantly assessed his surroundings, eyes flicking to Steve whenever he shifted. Steve had spent plenty of time around men like this, and he would have bet money that the man had a combat record. Even with the ski mask, Steve picked him as the one in the van who had been giving the orders—the man's build gave him away. His body language reassured Steve despite the gun; the man was alert but relaxed, and his finger wasn't on the trigger, but resting on the guard.

"Relax," the doctor said in a soothing voice. "You've been beaten very badly, but you will recover, given time and rest."

"Really? I hadn't noticed. I figured I must have fallen in the shower or something."

"Now, now. No need to be snide. I have been looking after you, after all."

"Sorry, being beaten like a rug has brought out the worst in me." He actually was sorry—mostly.

"You'll be back to your old self in no time. You really do have a remarkable constitution, Mr. Rogers."

Steve tensed.

"Who told you that name?"

"Don't worry, it's not a big secret. We do have televisions here."

"Fair enough. Steve is fine, anyway," Steve said. "And you are?"

"Clive will do," the doctor said. "And this is my friend . . . ah . . . Karl. Karl, you can take the mask off now."

"Thanks for that. I felt like an idiot with it on." Karl pulled off the mask, revealing rather sensitive and finely-drawn dark-brown features under a shaved skull. He smiled at Steve.

"I'm a big fan," Karl said. "So's the doc."

"Nice to meet you both. So why am I in here, behind a barred door, if you're both such big fans? It isn't very hospitable."

"Just a precaution," Clive said soothingly. "We didn't know what state of mind you might be in when you woke up, and we didn't want any . . . misunderstandings."

"How long have I been out?" Steve asked.

"Almost a day," the doctor replied. "Twenty hours, to be precise. I don't think you were ever in any real danger, but I took the precaution of putting you on a drip to keep your fluids up, and keeping you sedated until your vital signs leveled out."

"Well, I can't imagine how I could feel worse than I do

right now, but I appreciate your help, doctor," Steve said. "I owe you one. I hope we don't end up on different sides— that would be distressing for both of us."

The man with the gun laughed.

"Now, that's how you deliver a threat without being so crass as to come out and say it," he said. "Very classy."

"I don't make threats," Steve said. "I find I don't need to."

"Please, gentlemen," the doctor said. "Let's not get off on the wrong foot. Steve, we're on the same side. We want what you want."

"And what's that?" Steve asked. "What is it that you think I want?"

"Like you, we want to keep Katherine safe. She has something that we want very much, and we want to make sure that it doesn't end up in the wrong hands." Clive smiled. "So, we can be friends, no?"

"Let's just say not enemies for now . . . no?" Steve replied. "So, where is Katherine?"

"She's fine, she's upstairs talking to Gary," Clive replied. Noting Steve's look of enquiry, he explained. "Gary is our leader, if you'd call it that. More of a first among equals."

"I want to see her," Steve said. "I want to know that she's okay."

"You need to rest," the doctor said. "You aren't being kept from her, but there's only so much the body can take, even yours."

"I'll be the judge of that," Steve said.

Slowly, ignoring the pain that swept through his body in an incandescent wave, Steve got out of the bed. With a supreme act of will, he straightened, unwilling to let the other men see how weak he was. Karl was expressionless—though a grudging respect lurked in his eyes—but the doctor looked flabbergasted.

"I never would have believed it possible," he said. "Well, Mr. Rogers, if you feel up to it, we'll take you to see Katherine."

Steve dressed slowly, trying not to betray how much pain he was in, but every so often he would gasp as a stitch pulled or a muscle stretched against a sprain. Finally, the ordeal was over and Steve was fully dressed in reasonably well-fitting clothes, wrung out and feeling weaker than he'd ever been, even before the serum had changed him. The three men walked toward the door, Steve stumbling slightly a few steps from the bed. He felt a strong hand take his elbow, holding him steady. He tried to pull away, but the grip was too strong.

"Steady, Steve," Karl said. "It's okay, everyone needs a helping hand sometimes. Nothing to be ashamed of."

Steve relaxed and let the other man assist him. The corridor was as bare as the room had been, the walls no more than brushed concrete with a few safety lamps bolted to them. There were a number of doors that opened on empty rooms. Some were outfitted in the same sparse manner as Steve's, while others seemed almost luxurious in comparison, with furniture and even carpeting. Steve wondered what the criteria for getting one of those rooms were, and decided it didn't really matter.

They reached an elevator at the end of the hall and Steve let out a sigh of relief. He hadn't relished the thought of stairs at all. The ride up was silent—Steve had no breath to spare on conversation, and the other two men didn't seem to be in a talkative mood. The view as they stepped out of the elevator was a stark contrast to floor they had come up from. It was an airy office space, with open-plan desks and tasteful art prints. It could have been any of a thousand IT companies catering to the city's business interests.

"A front for the organization?" Steve asked the other men.

"In a way," the doctor replied. "But it more than pays for itself—the business is actually rather profitable."

"We attract some of the best and brightest coders and programmers in the business," a voice said. "It puts us in a great deal of demand, and all the money goes toward our other work."

The man speaking was dressed in a conservatively-cut business suit, his attire strikingly at odds with his long, black hair and bushy beard, and giving him the look of a lion that had dressed up to allay the fears of the animals around him. He had strong features and a curved beak of a nose, but it was his eyes that concerned Steve. They burned with a fire he had seen before—that of the fanatic utterly committed to his cause. Religion, politics, race—whatever the cause was, this was a man who would sacrifice anything to advance it. Or anyone.

"Please, Mr. Rogers, come this way," the man said. "Katherine is waiting in the boardroom, and I want to tell you all about the work we do here."

Steve followed the man into a boardroom dominated by a long table with a large plasma screen at one end. Smaller screens were built into the table itself, each with a small set of controls and a microphone on a flexible stem that was set in front of a leather chair.

Katherine sat at the far end of the table, playing on her phone. Their entrance caught her eye, and when she looked up and saw Steve, she bounced to her feet and almost ran the length of room. She moved to throw her arms around him, then got a good look at him and her arms fell to her sides.

"You look awful, Steve." She sounded as if she was about to burst into tears. "Are you okay?"

"I'll survive," Steve said. "But thanks for being considerate and not squeezing; I think that might have broken me."

As awful as he felt, he was relieved to see that Katherine looked unharmed. In fact, she looked as relaxed as he had ever seen her.

"So what have you been doing for last twenty hours?" he asked.

"While you've been lazing around in bed, you mean?" she teased. "Gary has been telling me all about their work. It's pretty amazing."

Steve didn't like the note of admiration he heard in her voice, but he didn't say anything. Oblivious, Katherine continued talking.

"And I've been talking to Karl—I think you two are going to get along. He's fascinating—he's been to about a hundred different countries, and he was in the Army."

Karl coughed behind Steve. "Ah, Marines actually."

"Oh, okay." She didn't seem very embarrassed by the correction. "Kind of the same thing, right?"

Steve and Karl shared a look of mutual understanding.

"Very much not the same thing," Steve said. "Neither really like getting mixed up with the other at all."

"You can say that again, Steve," Karl said. "Marines eat you Army boys for breakfast." He grinned as he said it, and tipped Steve a wink.

"Right now, I think even a Marine could eat me for breakfast," Steve said. "About the closest they'd get to an easy fight, anyway."

"Oh, burn," Karl said.

Katherine was looking at them both strangely.

"Are you two boys finished?"

The two men laughed.

"Yeah, I think so," Steve said. "So, what have you found out?"

"How about you let me present the information to Mr. Rogers?" Gary cut in. "Let him process it the way you did."

Steve expected Katherine to object, but instead she just nodded.

"Sounds good, Gary."

Gary strode to the rear of the boardroom and stood in front of the screen. He surveyed the room as if it were a crowd of hundreds, rather than just the few people currently present.

"Welcome to the Freedom Foundation. Our mission is twofold. On a political level, we oppose all forms of internet regulation, with the underlying philosophy that information should be free and that no government should be trusted to control its flow. Part of this is supporting political candidates whose positions align with ours, advertising, and championing appropriate legislation. We also try and provide free and accessible technology to people in countries that don't have the infrastructure we take for granted."

He paused and surveyed the room.

"Secondly, where political means fail, we take more direct action. That might mean electronic espionage against agencies that support curtailing rights, or more physical campaigns."

"Like bombing politicians' campaign offices?" Steve asked.

Gary stopped and glared at him. Steve was taken aback by the look of rage that crossed the man's face before he composed himself and the mask of benign authority fell back down. He was obviously not used to being interrupted—or questioned.

"Sometimes these things are necessary. No one has been harmed by anything we've done, and the cause justifies a few gutted offices."

"I've heard that line of thinking before," Steve said "And it never ends well."

"I can't remember asking for your approval," Gary replied. "If I recall correctly, it was my men who rescued you, and my doctor who patched you up."

"And we appreciate it, we really do," Katherine said. "I think Steve just wants to make sure no one is going to get hurt. Right, Steve?"

Rogers grunted noncommittally, but didn't interrupt again as Gary ran through the Freedom Foundation manifesto. It was standard activist group language, and after the first five minutes or so, Steve zoned him out. Instead, Rogers thought through ways of getting out of this place when the time came. He knew that he would have to wait until he was in better shape, but he now had a new concern, one that made time a precious commodity.

Katherine was listening with shining eyes. The fact that she was so obviously enthralled by the speech, despite having heard it before, told Steve that Gary had really done a number on her. There was no doubting that the man was charismatic, but Steve had become immune to magnetic personalities a long time ago.

Gary had stopped talking and was now looking at Steve expectantly.

"Look, Gary, this is all beyond me. I'm simply here with Katherine, so whatever she wants to do is fine with me," Steve said, playing the dumb grunt act for all he was worth. "But I will say that I'm grateful for you taking us in, and for the medical attention."

"Yes, thank you," Katherine chimed in.

"And you're running an impressive operation here, no doubt about it," Steve said.

Gary seemed mollified. "I'm sure that, the more you learn about us, the closer you will come to seeing our point of view, rather than having to rely on Katherine to form your opinions for you."

"I'm sure that's right," Steve said.

"Karl, how about you take Mr. Rogers on a tour? Tell him about your background—I think you have lots in common. He'll listen to you."

Karl nodded. "Sure, Gary. What about the girl?"

"Katherine, do you mind staying here with me? I want

to know a bit more about your research so we can plan how we're going to best use it for the cause."

"Sure thing," Katherine said. "I'm really excited about the possibilities, assuming we do decide to work together."

"Karl, don't keep Steve too long," Clive said, cutting off Gary before he could speak. "He really does need his rest. Let me know when you're done and I'll give him another check over before he goes back to bed."

"No worries, doc," Karl said cheerfully. "I'll try not to wear him out too much. C'mon Steve, I'll take you on the grand tour."

"Can we start with a coffee first?" Steve asked. "And some food, if that's possible?"

"Not a problem—we'll start in the cafeteria and then go from there." Karl stood and gestured for Steve to follow.

Steve pulled himself out of the chair, using the armrests for leverage. He thought he might already be slightly stronger, but when you were as weak as he currently was, it was hard to tell, and any improvement was strictly relative. But he was up, and shuffling out the door. On the way past, he tried to catch Katherine's eyes, but she was already talking to Gary, her expansive gestures betraying her enthusiasm. Steve sighed; it was going to be a struggle to get her away from this place when the time came, even if he was strong enough. But, just like how he was going to get in touch with

Maria, that was a problem for the future. Like any experienced veteran, Steve knew that he should eat while he had the chance and leave the rest of his problems for the future.

Chapter 10

The food in the cafeteria was surprisingly good considering that it was the middle of the weekend. The coffee machine looked like it was close to becoming self-aware, and had far too many buttons for Steve to even think about trying to operate it. But Karl had played it like a piano, and the resulting cup of coffee was one of the best that Steve had ever had. The two men sat down at one of the tables, sizing each other up. The Uzi was gone, but Steve noticed the other man still carried a handgun. From the brief look that Steve got, it was a Glock of some sort, probably a Glock 19, but he wasn't sure. Of course, the exact model didn't matter, it would still do the same job. Steve took the change in firearms to mean that the other man had decided he liked Steve enough that he didn't need the threat of the Uzi, but that he took his job seriously enough that he wouldn't bend enough to go unarmed. It didn't bother Steve; in fact, he respected someone who was that conscientious.

"So, the Marines," Steve said.

"Yeah," Karl replied. "Ten years, give or take."

"Decent hitch these days," Steve said. "Can I ask where you served?"

"I was a computer tech. Data retrieval specialist, to be precise."

Steve looked at him surprise, taking in the man's air of readiness and physical fitness.

"Please don't take this as denigrating support personnel in any way at all, because I know how much work they do," Steve said. "But you really don't have the look of someone who sat behind a desk."

"Oh, no, I didn't. Just the opposite, actually—I was in the Raiders."

Steve whistled softly. The Raiders were the Marines' elite. They'd sprung out of the reorganization of Force Recon and had a reputation for skill and toughness. If Karl had been a Raider, he'd be even more formidable than he looked.

"I haven't had a chance to work with you boys yet, but funnily enough, back in the '40s I did some operations with the original Marine Raiders—you know, the ones your regiment is named after."

"That's right," Karl said.

"They were top notch soldiers, and from everything I've heard, you men are worthy of the name."

"Thank you, sir, that means a lot coming from you,"

Karl said, shoulders straightening slightly. "There are battle honors in our mess hall wall that were captured on some of those missions."

"Enough with the 'sir,' Karl," Steve said. "So, what was a computer tech doing in the Raiders?"

"These days, everyone is using the internet. Terrorists have Twitter accounts and recruiting websites, and they use the dark web to send messages and transfer funds."

"The dark web?"

"The part of the internet that lies beneath the surface, that your average user never sees. It's where you can find anything you want, no matter how depraved. You can buy drugs, browse child pornography, recruit people for your cause—whatever it might be. It's a cesspit, the dark side of the golden age of information."

"It doesn't matter what we create, does it? There's always some way of turning it to evil. Splitting the atom could have powered the whole world—instead we used it to blow things up," Steve said. He didn't even want to mention the way that people had tried to duplicate the serum that had created him, not to help the sick, but to create their own super soldiers to serve their own evil purposes.

"You're right. But the bad guys' reliance on technology also gives the good side a weapon to use against them. If you can get access to that information, then you can break their backs," Karl explained. "Every time there was a raid or a deep-cover extraction, or anything like that, it became standard operating procedure to have a guy like me along. If we couldn't bring whatever computers there were back with us, I had to try and get into them as quickly as possible, and siphon out what data I could."

"Long way from a desk of your own."

"You bet. I hacked computers for fun when I was a kid. It was a game among the crowds I hung out with in high school and college, and we would have races or allocate points depending on what data you could get your hands on. But when you're in some cave in the Afghan mountains with dead bodies piled up around you, or the sound of machine-gun fire getting closer, it doesn't seem so fun anymore. And the penalties for failure aren't just suspension or even a jail sentence—they're people dying because you took too long, or another terrorist attack that could have been stopped with the information you failed to retrieve."

"I may not know much about computers, but I know how that feels. It's a heavy burden to carry," Steve said. "I'm surprised you want anything to do with computers now. You must hate them."

"No!" Steve was surprised by the other man's vehemence. "I love computers. I love the internet. I just hate what people use them for. But the good they do, what they're capable of doing in the right hands . . . well, you would never believe me if I tried to explain."

"You'd be surprised. Why don't you try me?"

"I was one of the Raiders' first recruits; before that, I was in Force Recon. I've been on missions to more countries than I can count. I've done tours—some official, some completely off the books—in the Middle East, Central America, Eastern Europe. And in that time, I've seen how the information age is changing the world. The Arab Spring was just the start. Freedom of information, freedom of communication—they're nails in the coffin of any totalitarian regime. Katherine has given me the rough outline of her research, and I can tell you right now, it's going to change the world. It shouldn't belong to any government; it should belong to the people."

Steve felt a stab of jealousy that Katherine had already shared so much with the young man sitting across from him. He fought it down, knowing it was unworthy.

"So how did you end up here?" Steve asked.

"I had planned on making a career of the Marines, but . . ." Karl paused for a moment. "Everyone has a breaking point, where they've seen too much, done too much."

Steve nodded. He knew exactly what Karl meant.

"So, eventually I resigned my commission. I had no idea what I was going to do, but I wasn't too worried. I had plenty of benefits built up and a nice little nest egg to live off of. Part of the process when I left the Marines was seeing a doctor. Even when the physical injuries healed, there were things I still needed to work through. That's how I met Clive. After the first few appointments, we just started talking, you know, the usual stuff, sports and all that. He may look like an egghead, but he played college ball—he just wasn't big enough to go pro. Anyway, we bonded over that, and then one day I'd just read an article about net neutrality and I was bit steamed up and wanted to talk about that. Turned out we had similar views on the subject."

"So he recruited you?"

"Eventually. After a few months in rehab, I decided I needed to find a job. He suggested I try Freetech—that's the legitimate business here. With my background, I was qualified enough, that's for sure." Karl laughed. "Turned out my other qualifications were just as desirable. Gary took a personal interest in me and eventually invited me to join the Foundation. Once they were sure they could trust me, he asked me to act as head of security. Unofficially, of course."

"And you lead the raids?" Steve asked.

"Yeah, and do all the planning. I told Gary that I was only willing to be part of it if we had a strict no collateral damage policy. I've seen too many political groups that think the ends justify the means, and that don't care if people get hurt. So we only choose targets where we know no one could get caught up in it."

"And what did Gary think of that?" Steve asked carefully.

"He was fine with it, of course." There was something in Karl's voice, a note of defensiveness.

"Are you sure about that, Karl?" Steve asked. "Sometimes these civilians who've never seen action don't really understand the consequences—like what it looks like after a bomb has gone off. It's all theoretical to them."

"Okay, maybe Gary can be a bit . . . enthusiastic. But it's just that he's passionate about what we're doing. He believes in the importance of our cause," Karl said. "Once I've explained things to him, he calms down and we do it my way. That's my job."

"And what if you weren't here to calm him down?" Steve asked softly.

"I am, so it doesn't matter," Karl said, a bit sullenly. "Anyway, the truth is that Gary is great on ideas, but not so much on the execution. I don't think he would be doing much of anything if it weren't for Clive and me. Clive is the administrative genius that keeps the lights on, and I'm the muscle."

Steve didn't say anything. He thought that Gary might be a bit more dangerous than Karl gave him credit for, but he knew that saying anything would be counterproductive. Karl was obviously devoted to the man who had given him a new purpose in life.

At a slight buzzing noise, Karl touched a finger to his ear to activate the transceiver nestled there. Steve could see the change that came over his face as he listened to whatever the voice at the other end was saying, the friendliness leeching away and leaving a lack of emotion that told Steve all he needed to know. Karl the conversationalist was gone, and Steve was now facing the head of security.

"Sir, I'm afraid that I'm going to have to ask you to return to the basement with me."

"And if I don't want to?" Steve asked calmly.

"I'm afraid that I have to insist, sir. It's for your own safety." Karl placed his hand on the butt off his gun. "We'll both be a lot happier if you just come along without making a fuss, that's all."

Steve tensed, ready to launch himself at the other man, then thought better of it as another wave of pain washed through him. He simply wasn't in any shape to resist. Instead, he raised both hands, although even that movement provoked a stabbing pain. He was relieved that it seemed be much less severe than what the same movement would have brought with it even few hours ago. His accelerated healing was working its wonders, and he was starting to believe that he might be close to his peak within a day or so. For now, though, he needed to play it safe.

"Lead on, Karl," he said.

The other man gave him a sardonic grin. "Oh, I think I should let you go first, don't you?"

Steve shrugged and moved toward the door. He made sure he gave Karl plenty of room on the way past.

"You know the way, right?" Karl called from behind him. "Straight to the elevator."

"Yeah," Steve replied. "I think I can find my way."

He deliberately took his time, exaggerating his shuffling steps, stopping from time to time to lean against the wall and catch his breath. At least, most of it was exaggerated, but he still breathed a sigh of relief each time he was able to stop. To his credit, Karl showed no signs of impatience, letting Steve take all the time he needed. He even encouraged Steve to take a seat halfway along the corridor, and helped him in and out of it. The only thing that betrayed their new dynamic was the gun in Karl's hand when he stepped into the elevator to join Rogers. They both pointedly ignored it on the way down, two professionals making the best of a bad situation.

Karl waited in the elevator until Steve was fully out, then joined him in the corridor. Steve walked toward the room in which he had awoken, but Karl stopped him.

"No, not that one."

"Huh?" Steve said, startled. "Have I got an upgrade or something?"

"That was just one of the medical holding rooms. We keep them as sterile as we can for when we're providing sanctuary for people who have been injured, or who are sick. We have much nicer digs set up for you. Third door on the left."

This room was much nicer than his original lodgings; it had carpet and a TV, as well as two twin beds. A door in the corner led to a small en suite, and a bookshelf took up most of one of the walls. Katherine was lying on one of the beds, reading a book. When she saw him, she dropped it and sat up.

"Steve!"

"Hi, Katherine," he replied, shuffling into the room.

He heard the door swing shut behind him, and the sound of bolts clicking into place, but he didn't even look around. He'd been expecting it, after all. He walked over to the unoccupied bed, still slowly, but without the exaggerated shuffle from the cafeteria, and lowered himself onto it, using the bed frame as a support.

"What's going on?" Katherine asked. "What did you do?"

"What do you mean, what did I do?" Steve said. "Karl and I were having a lovely chat when all of a sudden he got a message from your friend, Gary, and then next thing I knew, I was on my way down here."

"He's not my friend," Katherine said. "What's that supposed to mean?"

"You seemed awfully taken with him when he was giving his little speech earlier," Steve said. "You looked like you were loving what he had to say."

"Seriously, Steve? Have you never heard the expression 'you catch more flies with honey'?"

"What?" Steve asked.

"He's the sort of guy who loves the sound of his own voice, and especially loves it when people validate his own high opinion of himself. I picked that up straightaway. I want to think that he doesn't reflect on the rest of the people here, but it does worry me that someone like him is the leader. I've been trying to work out whether we can trust them despite Gary, so I've been playing the role of impressionable young woman—and he's been lapping it up."

"Oh," Steve said. "It's just . . . well, you were very convincing."

"Of course I was. That's the thing with being a young female in tech circles—you're constantly underestimated by the men around you. I hate it, but it's something that you learn to use to your own advantage," she said. "Geez, Steve, I would have thought you know me better than that by now. I won't lie, I'm a little hurt."

Steve felt a little ashamed of himself. "Sorry, okay? I'm not really at my best right now."

"Yeah, I can tell. You still look like crap." There was concern in her voice, which he supposed was better than the hurt of just a minute ago. "Are you going to be okay? I mean, seriously, you look terrible."

"You'd be surprised how much damage I can take. Not that I want to go through it again anytime soon. Just give me a day or so, and I'll be as good as new."

"Okay." She sounded doubtful, but didn't pursue it. "So, why do you think we're down here now?"

"I was hoping you could tell me. Did you say anything to Gary that might have made him think you weren't going to cooperate with his grand vision? I think that's the sort of thing that might have pushed him over the edge."

"I don't think he's that bad, Steve."

"I'm not sure that's true," he replied. "Be that as it may, was there anything that might have triggered this?"

"No! We were just talking about our favorite operating system of all things, and then his mobile rang. He went down to the end of the room to answer it. He didn't say much, not that I could make out, just 'yeahs' and 'uh-huhs.' When he hung up, he was almost a different person. Completely unresponsive, just brushed off my questions and told me that he needed me to go down to the basement for my own good. When I protested, he called in one of the other security guys—you know, the ones who picked us up?"

Steve nodded and she went on.

"He was really polite the whole time, but he made it really clear my only option was going along with Gary's instructions. I didn't want to force their hand—those guns look awfully nasty—so I just did what they said."

"Good idea," Steve said.

"So what do we do now?" she asked. "Do you have some sort of cunning plan to get us out?"

"No, sorry, nothing for now. I'm certainly not in any shape to be busting down doors. What's the book selection like?"

"Not too bad, I guess. Why do you ask?"

"Since all we can do is wait and find out what's going on, I'm going to grab a book and relax, and wait for them to come down and give us some answers," Steve said. "Obviously that phone call has something to do with it, but that's all we know for now, so there's no point in worrying about it."

"How can you be so relaxed about this?" she asked.

"When you've been in as many cells as I have, you get a bit casual about it all," Steve said. "And this one is pretty nice as these places go. At least there's something to keep us occupied. Speaking of which . . ."

"What? Oh." Katherine jumped up and went over to the bookshelf. "What do you feel like? There are some more of those books you were into at the cabin. The ones with the colors in the name."

"That'll do nicely!"

Katherine passed him a book and he settled in to wait.

Chapter 11

It was the next morning before they came for Steve and Katherine. There were no smiles this time, and Karl looked grim as he gestured with the gun in his hand. He'd gone back to the Uzi again, which told Steve all he needed to know about the situation. Karl rebuffed any attempts at conversation on the way to the elevator, and it was only after the doors slid shut behind him that he turned to face them.

"Cap, one piece of advice. Just tread carefully—I don't want things getting out of hand. It's not going to help anyone—especially not her—if you do something stupid."

"What do you mean, 'getting out of hand'?" Steve asked, but Karl wouldn't say any more and ignored their questions. Steve focused on a brief self-inventory, trying to decide if he was strong enough to make a break for it—and reluctantly deciding he wasn't.

When they got to the boardroom, Gary and Clive were

with three strangers. The newcomers were all dressed in expensive business suits, but underneath they were all lean, whipcord muscle and deadly grace. Two of the strangers deferred to the third with every action and word, waiting for him to speak, and keeping between him and everyone else in the room. Their leader, for that was obviously was what he was, had a beard to rival Gary's, but where Gary was a lion, this man was a leopard. Even in repose he seemed to be full of coiled energy, ready to leap into explosive action. His eyes passed over Steve with little interest, but when he saw Katherine, they lit up like a man who has seen water after crawling through a burning desert. It was nothing sexual; more like a man whose dreams are finally within reach of his grasp after years of yearning.

"This is the girl?" he asked Gary. "The one with the knowledge we need?"

His voice had the harsh inflections of far Eastern Europe, but his diction was absolutely perfect, bespeaking a very expensive education.

"I'm Katherine, thanks for asking," she said. "Gary, who are these men? They seem to know who I am, so introductions are in order, don't you think?"

Gary flushed. "I was getting to that, Katherine. No need to be like that."

The other man was looking at him with amused contempt. "Who is in charge here? I thought it was you, Gary."

Gary ignored them. "Steve, Katherine, this is Ernst. Ernst, you might know Mr. Rogers better as Captain America."

He smiled at the look of surprise on Ernst's face.

"Please forgive Mr. Rogers, Ernst. He isn't himself; he's carrying a number of wounds. In fact, it's a relief to see you even walking, Steve," Gary said. "I'll let Ernst tell you about himself."

Gary didn't bother introducing the other two men, which would have told Steve all he needed to know if it hadn't already been obvious—they were simply bodyguards; muscle beneath Gary and Ernst's notice.

"I represent the Temasikian Liberation Front. Perhaps you've heard of us."

"I've heard of you, all right," Steve said grimly.

Depending on what you thought about the morality of collateral damage, it was a matter of debate whether the Temasikian Liberation Front were freedom fighters or terrorists. The Temasikian Liberation Front, or TLF as most media found it much easier to call them, had a reputation for not being too picky about their targets. It only muddied the waters that the government they were dedicated to overthrowing was one of the most despotic in the world, with a human rights record that would make even most dictators blanch. To Steve, that still didn't justify the TLF's methods, but for plenty of people, it went a long way toward doing so.

Ernst ignored Steve's tone. "We've been struggling against the oppression of our people for years now. But we are fighting against the full resources of our government, and every year it seems like there are fewer of us willing to make the ultimate sacrifice. But that's not even our greatest obstacle—we are fighting an information war. We rely on our friends in the West for money and weapons, but the oppressors only allow their side of events to see the light of day, and they are slowly turning the world against us."

"Information is power," Gary said, nodding. "Isn't that what I've been saying all these years?"

"Our nation doesn't have the same infrastructure as many others do; our only connection to the outside world is controlled by the government, and the terrain in our country makes wireless solutions less effective than we require. All those mountains and valleys play havoc with reception." Ernst said. "We can tap into the government network, but we just can't utilize it the way we need to."

"Hence your interest in me," Katherine said.

"Yes, that's right," Ernst said. "When Gary told us of your unique research, it was an answer to our prayers."

"Wait, Gary told you?" Steve asked. He glared at the other man.

"What? I've been in touch with the TLF for a long time now. The situation in their country is a classic example of a government trying to control the flow of information, and using the power they have to do so as a tool of oppression. Those people have a right to unfiltered access to the outside world, and we've been trying to help the TLF make that happen."

"And when Katherine came along, it seemed liked the perfect opportunity, right?" Steve asked. "She has the answers that they've been looking for?"

"Exactly," Gary said. "This is the moment we've been waiting for, to strike a genuine blow for freedom."

"What's this 'we'?" Steve snapped. "You didn't have anything to do with any of this. It's Katherine's research, Katherine's decision."

"Thanks, Steve, I appreciate that—but how about letting me speak for myself?" Katherine said. "I'm getting a bit sick of everyone talking around me like I'm not here."

"That's not how I meant it," Steve said.

"I know, but just let me talk, okay?" Her expression softened. "I know you mean well, Steve."

Gary looked smug until Katherine rounded on him.

"How dare you, Gary? I didn't tell you about my research so you could go telling everyone. I mean seriously, I don't care if it is some international resistance group, you're no better than some high school kid blabbing someone's secrets."

Steve stifled a chuckle. Gary looked like he had bitten into a lemon—it had probably been a long time since anyone had spoken to him like that. A look over at Ernst wiped the smile off Steve's face, however—the other man looked furious at the interruptions. Fanatics rarely had a sense of humor, in Steve's experience.

"Look, Katherine," Gary said. "These men have come a very long way. You aren't going to send them away empty handed, are you?"

"I don't care how far they've travelled, Gary. I'm not going to be pressured into anything simply by you putting me on the spot. That's not how it works."

Ernst opened his mouth to speak, but shut it as Gary shook his head his head at him.

Gary spread his hands in placatory gesture. "You're right, Katherine, I should never have put you in this position. I apologize."

"Well, thank you, Gary," Katherine said. She sounded slightly mollified, but nowhere near completely happy.

"Will you at least think about it, Katherine?" Gary asked. "Can you do that?"

Katherine looked over at Steve.

"Can we have some privacy, Gary?" she asked. "I'd like to discuss this with Steve."

"What is this?" Ernst snapped. "Gary, we—"

"Ernst. Not now." There was a tone of command in Gary's voice that Steve hadn't heard before and, for perhaps the first time, he was able to understand how Gary had been able to attract the loyalty of men like Karl. Ernst subsided, looking slightly surprised at himself for doing so.

"How about we clear the room and give these two a few moments," Gary said. "Can we do that, Ernst?"

The other man nodded grudgingly, and Gary gestured to the others. As they filed out, Gary turned.

"I hope you'll do the right thing, Katherine. I know you believe the same things we do."

He closed the door softly behind him, leaving Steve and Katherine sitting across from each other. Steve grabbed a pitcher of water and poured them both a glass. He took a sip, using the time to muster his thoughts, and pushed a glass across to Katherine. She took it with a smile.

"You aren't seriously thinking about going with them, are you?" Steve asked. "There are no good guys in that war; that man has blood on his hands. A lot of blood."

"And what if I say yes? Are you going to try and stop me?" she asked. "You promised you would respect my decision." She gave him a mock solemn look. "Captain America isn't going to break his word is he?"

"I . . . I . . ." Steve sputtered, then grinned despite himself. "You've got me there, I guess. But, seriously, are you?"

"Of course not," Katherine said. "I'm not stupid. But something tells me that Ernst is not the sort of man to take no for an answer."

"That's what I'm worried about," Steve said. "I'm not sure what I can do about it if he decides to fight. I'm still not fully recovered. I need at least another day or so before I'll be even close."

"Maybe we can stall for time? Put them off until you're fully recovered?"

"We can try," Steve said doubtfully. "We might have to try and work out a way of getting them to believe you're thinking about agreeing." He leaned forward and put his hand over one of hers. "You need to understand something, though. Don't make the mistake of thinking these men are idiots, Katherine. You don't survive as long as they have doing what they do without becoming a very good judge of character, or knowing when someone is lying to you."

"What else can we do but try?" Katherine asked. "I don't know what else to do."

"I really don't know. Are you ready?" At her nod, Steve rose from his seat and went to the doorway. He leaned out and yelled to the other men. "Okay, we're done."

Gary waited until everyone was seated, and then turned to Katherine.

"So, what did you decide?"

"Gary, we've talked about this stuff. You know how I feel about electronic freedoms, and I sympathize with what the TLF is trying to achieve. But let's be honest, there is some baggage there that makes me uneasy about getting involved."

"Are you saying no?" Ernst asked.

"I'm just saying that I'd like to think about it some more,

that's all. After all, you're asking me to travel halfway across the world."

"I'm sure that Ernst and his friends can wait a little on your decision," Gary said. "Right, Ernst?"

"No!" Ernst was on his feet, hands clenched at his sides. "We can't wait. Every minute we are sitting here is another minute my people are suffering. Gary, I want what we agreed upon, and I want it now."

Steve pushed himself to his feet, trying not to let on how much the effort cost him, hoping he could bluff the other man.

"What you agreed on?" he asked coldly. "What have you promised these men, Gary?"

Gary hesitated, looking from Karl to Clive. His mouth worked as he searched for something to say, but nothing came out.

Ernst laughed. "They don't know? It's very simple. The girl will come and help the cause, and we will transfer $5 million to the Freedom Foundation. We may have a shortage of freedom, but we have no shortage of precious gems and metals. Why else do you think the West has never dared interfere too much with our government? They don't want to kill the golden goose."

The looks of shock on Karl and Clive's faces were too raw to be faked. Steve knew that this was the first they were hearing of this arrangement. Somehow, it made him feel a little better knowing that they hadn't been in on it; he liked both men, and he felt a bond with Karl that stemmed from their shared service.

"I came to you because I thought that you were fighting for a cause," Katherine shouted. "Is money all that matters to you?"

"Katherine, it's not money for its own sake; just think of the good we can do with it," Gary said defensively. "And it's not even the important part. The oppression of the Temasikian people is exactly what we're fighting against."

"It's not what I'm fighting against," Clive said, a look of disdain on his face. "If she wanted to go with them, that would be one thing. It's the kind of scenario we've been hoping for. If it was a piece of technology we were talking about, it might be different, but there is no way in hell I'm being part of selling someone off as if they were some sort of property. We're done." He stood and walked out of the room, not looking back even when Gary called out to him.

Gary buried his face in his hands, then looked up. "What about you, Karl? Are you going to walk out on me? Are you going to try and stop this from happening?"

"I don't think there's anything I can do about it at this point," Karl said.

Gary followed Karl's gaze to where the two TLF bodyguards were standing, guns drawn and covering the rest of the room. Karl's fingers twitched as if he were considering going for his Uzi, but better sense prevailed, and he let his hand fall to his side.

"Ernst?" Gary said, and, at the note of almost childlike bewilderment in his voice, Steve almost felt sorry for him. Almost.

It was amazing how quickly the balance of power in the room had shifted. Steve had seen this before—someone who had stood at the sidelines and had never had a loaded gun pointed at them before wilting at the cold, hard reality of the proximity of death. The threat had shaken Gary's sense of the way the world worked to its foundations, and something inside him had broken.

"Surely we can talk about this?" Gary asked plaintively.

Ernst had drawn his own gun, but, for now at least, it was still pointed at the ground. It wasn't the sort of weapon you argued with, either—it was an Israeli-manufactured Desert Eagle, chambered for .50 Action Express cartridges—the sort of gun that could punch holes through walls. Flesh and bone had no chance.

"Talk? That's all men like you every do, talk and talk, while our children are dying. You prattle on about freedom, but you have no idea how good you have it, or how soft you really are." Ernst spat on the ground. "I don't have that luxury. I am not leaving without what I came for. You can take your five million, or you can stand on principle, but either way, she is coming with us."

Steve dove at Ernst's legs in attempt bring him down, but the other man pivoted and swung his pistol down on the back of Steve's head. Steve lay on the ground for a moment, dizzy and hurting, but more embarrassed than anything by his poor attempt. If he hadn't been so injured, he would have dealt with Ernst in a heartbeat, before taking care of the other two men, but right now he felt worse than useless. He struggled to his feet and readied himself for another charge, not caring about the gun in the other man's hand, just desperate to do something, anything.

He was pulled up short by a strong arm wrapping around his neck, and the muzzle of a gun pressing into his back. He tensed, trying to find some leverage, but the man holding him was too strong.

"That's far enough," Karl said loudly, before lowering his voice so that only Steve could hear him. "Don't be stupid. This isn't going to help Katherine."

"It seems your man has more sense than you, Gary," Ernst said. "Don't you?"

"Take the money, boss. At least that way we get something out of this snafu." Karl's arm was like iron, not giving an inch against Steve's renewed struggles. His whisper was a hiss in Steve's ear. "Just relax. Trust me, we'll work something out. You're no good to anyone dead."

"Gary, you can't be serious. Please," Katherine said. "You can't let them do this."

Gary didn't say anything, unable to even meet her eyes.

"It's out of Gary's hands," Steve said. "And he knows it. This is what happens when you get in too deep. You shouldn't have tried playing with the big boys, Gary."

"Shut up."

"So, one person can lose their freedom and that's okay, Gary? The greater good and all that? I guess when it comes to the cause, one girl doesn't really matter. I have to admire your principles, Gary, you're a real sweet guy."

"Shut up!"

"Are you going to be able to live with this, Gary?" Steve taunted.

"I said shut up," Gary screamed, spittle flying. "Get him out of here, Karl. Take him back down to the basement and keep him there while I decide what to do with him."

"Steve?" Katherine said. "Don't let them take me away."

Rogers met her eyes. "Katherine, don't panic. I'll come and find you, no matter what. I promise. Okay?"

Katherine nodded.

"And when I do, Ernst and his friends are going to be very sorry."

Ernst pointed his gun at Steve and pulled back the hammer. The click sounded very loud in the sudden silence.

"Maybe I should take care of the problem now, save trouble later. You can't come after us with a bullet between your eyes." His finger tightened slowly. With the hammer cocked,

Steve knew there wasn't much pull at all on the trigger, and he braced himself. It was funny how, even when you knew that there was nothing you could do, the body still clung to any thin thread of self-preservation.

"I wouldn't recommend that," Karl said, his voice calm and even. "If you put a bullet in Captain America, they'll never stop coming after you. Not just law enforcement, but people who can knock down buildings around you. They won't care where you are, they'll come and find you, and then where will the cause be? Do you really need that static?"

Ernst gave Steve a considering look, then slowly let the hammer fall back into place. He holstered the gun and glared at Karl.

"You may be right," he said. "But get him out of my sight before I change my mind. I am rapidly losing patience."

Steve struggled as Karl frog-marched him out of the room, but he was still far too weak to do anything about it. Despite his protests, Karl dragged him down the hallway and hammered on the elevator's button, shifting anxiously until the doors opened and he could bundle Steve inside. The last thing he heard was Katherine calling out his name, and then the doors slid shut, cutting her pleas off and leaving only silence in their place.

Chapter 12

It was hard to keep track of time in the basement room. No windows let the sunlight in, and there was just the ever-present glare of the overhead lights. Steve filled the long wait by testing his body. Even in a bare room there are a number of exercises you can do, and Steve knew them all. Push-ups, sit-ups, jumping jacks, isometrics—he worked his way through them. Slowly, his body responded, each movement coming slightly easier than the previous one. The only time he paused his exertions was for the tray of food that was slid through a slot in the door at regular intervals, shoveling it down quickly and then resuming his workout. By his estimation, he had been in the room for about thirty-six hours when the door finally opened.

It was Karl, his handgun out and leveled at Steve. "How are you feeling, Captain?" He was careful to keep some distance between them, standing near the open door with Steve against the wall.

"I'd feel a lot better if I wasn't locked down here," Steve said. "And if Katherine wasn't up there."

He noticed the shift in Karl's eyes.

"Is she still up there, or have they taken her away?"

"That's why I'm here," Karl said. "They left about an hour ago."

Even with the gun in his hand, he took a step back at the anger in Steve's eyes.

"Hang on a second," Karl said. "I'm on your side."

"Are you, Karl? You have a gun, and you're between me and the door."

"Oh, this." He looked down at the gun, then clicked the safety back on before holstering it. "I wasn't sure you'd give me a chance to talk if I didn't have it."

"I'm listening," Steve said. "But not for long."

"After you left, some more of those TLF goons turned up. They were keeping a pretty close eye on us all, and every time I even looked like heading in this direction, one of them would follow me." He walked over and took a seat on the bed.

"They spent a fair bit of time running through some computer model with Katherine, demonstrating how effective that tool she created would be at defeating their government's firewall. I tell you what, Katherine is good—very good. I never would have come up with that solution. It's elegant."

"And then?"

"Well, Gary managed to regain some of his backbone, when it came to his money, at least. He wouldn't let Ernst leave with her until the wire transfer processed. Ernst tried to bluster his way out, but Gary pretty much threatened to call the cops if he tried to leave with Katherine. Gary said that he'd scupper the whole deal if he had to." Karl shook his head. "I guess that shows exactly where his real priorities are. I can't believe I bought the whole 'freedom is a right' line."

"You shouldn't blame yourself, Karl," Steve said. "We all need something to believe in."

"I guess so," Karl said, then changed the subject, as if embarrassed. "As soon as they left, Gary went back to his office, to brood or count his money or something, I don't know. I took the opportunity to head to the basement, and here I am."

"Here you are," Steve said. "But, why, exactly? Are you really willing to go against Gary? Weren't you his head of security?"

Karl grinned at him.

"Oh, I quit." His expression turned serious. "We've done some things in the name of our cause that are . . . legally questionable, but I've been able to live with them. But standing aside while a young woman is kidnapped is not something I can do. There wasn't anything I could do when I was so outgunned, especially not with you in the shape you were in. But whatever I can do to make this right, I will, and I think together we can get her back."

"Together?" Steve asked. "You're going to come with me?"

"Of course I am. That's what Marines do—bail you Army boys out."

Steve didn't dignify that with a reply.

"So, what's the plan?"

Karl handed Steve his shield. "Let's go see if we can convince Gary to tell us where they've taken Katherine. Hopefully, they're still in the country."

Steve's dismay must have shown on his face.

"Hey, Cap, don't worry. We'll get her back. Even if we have to go all the way to Temasikia. But it's not going to come to that—I've checked flights and we have at least a day. It's not exactly a boutique destination."

"Yeah, but there are plenty of other places for them to go. Let's get a move on—the sooner we get after them, the sooner we'll get her back."

The two men moved swiftly down the hall and took the elevator back up to the office level. The area was deserted, the lights turned out, and the only illumination coming from the green glow of exit signs.

"Follow me," Karl said.

They went past the boardroom and down another hallway. The last door was shut, a soft glow of light spilling out from underneath. Karl rapped on the door.

"Go away," Gary called from inside. "I'm busy."

"We need to talk, Gary," Karl said. "Let me in."

"Come back later, okay?"

"Not later. Now."

"I said no. Now leave me alone."

Karl turned the doorknob, but it was locked. He braced himself and kicked out, the sole of his foot hitting just below the door handle. It was only a cheap interior door, and the results were dramatic—with a smashing, splintering noise, the door went flying backward, coming off the bottom hinge and hanging there, swinging back and forth.

Gary sat at his desk, looking shocked. The desk was glass and chrome, in an L shape that shielded him from the rest of the room. The top was covered in trinkets, Lucite blocks with designs etched inside, and a scale model of a DNA double helix.

"What the . . ."

"I told you that we needed to talk, Gary," Karl said. "You should have listened."

Gary's eyes were locked on the door, and it took him a moment to realize that Steve was in the room, too. Steve wouldn't have thought it possible, but the other man's eyes widened even further.

"What is he doing here, Karl? I told you to keep him in the basement."

"I'm not taking orders from you anymore, Gary," Karl said. "You're going to listen to me."

"What are you talking about? You have to listen to me," Gary snapped. "I gave you a job, took you in. You owe me."

"It was never a job, Gary," Karl said. "Don't you think I could have found work anywhere I wanted? I was here because I believed in what we were doing; I believed in you. But how can I now, after you literally just sold someone?"

"It's not like that! You make it sound so . . . sordid. So mercenary."

"That's exactly what it is."

"No, no, the Temasikians need her. They deserve to be free. They've been oppressed for decades, what's a few months for Katherine? Once they've learned everything she has to teach them, they'll let her go," Gary's voice was pleading. "You have to understand."

"I understand far too well," Karl said. "I'm done with this conversation. And I'm done with you. Now, tell me where they are."

"I can't do that, Karl," Gary said.

"Yes, you can, Gary. This is your chance to make things right."

"Do you know what they'll do to me if I tell you?"

Steve leaped across the room and threw Gary's desk aside. Gary fell back in shock, his chair tipping over and spilling him onto the ground. He scuttled back against the wall, his hands held up as if to ward off a blow.

"What do you think I'm going to do to you if you don't tell me, Gary?" Steve said, his voice cold. "Where is she?"

Even in his terror, Gary wasn't stupid. He laughed weakly.

"You aren't going to kill me, Rogers. That's not your style. You can threaten me all you want—I know there's nothing you'll do that comes close to what Ernst will do."

Gary was right. He had called Steve's bluff. No matter what was at stake, he wouldn't—couldn't—torture information out of a man or kill him in cold blood. Gary knew that, and Steve knew that Gary knew that.

Steve had to come up with something, but all he could think about was Katherine and the clock winding down. His chain of thought was cut short by the sound of a pistol's action being racked.

"Gary." Karl's voice was flat and inflectionless. "Rogers may be constrained by his moral code, and don't get me wrong, I really admire that. But I feel no such compunction."

The gun bucked in Karl's hands with a roar. A neat hole appeared in the floor next to Gary's foot, and he let out a choked moan of fear. The gun barked again, and another hole appeared next to Gary's other foot.

"Wow, I am on fire today!" Karl said. "Can't believe how accurate this thing is. But I wouldn't count on it continuing,

Gary. I'd hate to put a bullet in your ankle. I've heard that is absolutely excruciating. I knew a guy who picked up one in a little flyspeck outside Mosul. Five surgeries and a lot of metal pins, and he still walks with a limp."

Gary whimpered and jerked again as Karl put a bullet in the wall next to him.

"So, what do you say, Gary? Are you going to tell us where they are?" Another shot. "Are they still in the country?" Another shot. "Have they flown out?" Another shot.

"Okay! Okay!" Gary blubbered. "They're still in the city. They're meeting with some arms dealers tomorrow, so you have at least until then."

"Where in the city?" Karl asked. "Give us a location."

"I don't know!" Gary almost yelled. "I swear."

The gun rang out again.

"Wait! I have a phone number. Just let me do a reverse look up on it. Oh."

All three of the men looked down at the wreckage of Gary's computer, lying among the remains of the desk. Karl grabbed Gary's arm and hauled him to his feet.

"Come with me." He half dragged, half marched Gary down the hallway and into another cubicle, looming over him as he logged into the computer.

"Okay, here it is." Gary scribbled an address on a piece of paper. "Now, please, let me go."

"Let you go? So you can sell us out to the TLF for a few more dollars and tell yourself you're doing it for freedom?" Karl said. "You make me sick."

Karl dragged Gary kicking and screaming down the corridor, all the way to the elevator. He bundled the other man into the elevator and hit the button for the basement. Despite Gary's pleas, Karl refused to speak, his eyes staring expressionlessly to the front, refusing to look at either Gary or Steve. He took Gary to the room where they had been holding Steve and threw him inside, slamming the door behind him and bolting it.

As soon as the door closed, Karl turned and vomited on the floor, bracing himself against a wall. He straightened up, wiped his mouth, and looked at Steve apologetically.

"Sorry, I'm not really cut out to be an interrogator. I thought I'd enjoy that, but it made me feel dirty."

"No need to be sorry, Karl," Steve said. "It'd worry me if you found that easy. I've seen people who do, who grow to enjoy it. It's a cancer that eats you up from the inside. A spiritual cancer."

Karl gave him weak smile. "Thanks, I feel a bit better now."

Steve looked at the address. "Okay, it's the other side of the city. We should make a move."

"What about weapons? I've got your gear, but other than

that, we don't have much of an arsenal here—just a few more machine pistols and some handguns. Plus a couple of tactical shotguns."

Steve grinned at Karl. "I don't think weapons are going to be one of our problems."

* * *

"Oh man. This is like Christmas. No, like every Christmas of my life rolled into one and times a thousand."

Karl looked like he didn't know where to start first. They were standing in a warehouse, surrounded on all sides by racks of weapons. He ran his hand over a display of handguns, and took out a nickel-plated Colt M1911A1 mounted with a laser sight. He picked it up and sighted down the barrel, watching the little dot spring into being, and tracing it along the wall.

"Can I just live here? Please? I won't eat much. Promise."

"Sorry, someone might notice you after a while," Steve said.

"So, how many of these places are there?" Karl asked.

"There's at least one in every major city," Steve said. "Any S.H.I.E.L.D. operative has access. It's very efficient, means you don't have to be carrying much around. You just come here as needed, grab the tools you need for the job at hand, and then when you're done, you return them. Not that they expect you sign every bullet in and out, they just ask that you be reasonable."

To get to the warehouse, Steve had directed Karl through the back streets of the city in the same van they'd met in days before. He had refused to answer any of Karl's questions, only assuring him that he was in for a surprise. The warehouse looked just like the dozen others on the narrow street in the heart of industrial sector, and Karl had thrown Steve a dubious look as they approached the door. It had seemed perfectly normal, a cheap lock on the hasp of the door, but Steve had ignored the lock, and instead opened the junction box on the wall next to the door. He pressed on the edge of the power board and it swung open to reveal a high-tech keypad. He punched in a series of numbers, eliciting a low click followed by a humming noise as the door slid upward into the roof, revealing another door, this one made of steel. Another click, and it swung open, and Steve gestured for Karl to follow him inside.

Steve let Karl have a look around for a few minutes, enjoying the man's childlike pleasure in the weapons on offer. But time was ticking away, and it was time to get to work. Steve walked over to another set of lockers and pulled out a drawer to reveal a jumble of assorted mobile phones. He picked one at random and switched it on, then punched in a number. Steve listened as it rang, until finally it cut off with a recorded message telling him the number he had called was unavailable. He tried again, then once more, with no better result. Thrusting the phone into his pocket with a frustrated snarl, he walked over and put his hand on Karl's shoulder. Karl turned away from the gun he was examining with a degree of reluctance, looking like a baby who had had his candy taken away.

"Sorry to interrupt, but how about you start grabbing some weapons? We need nonlethal rounds—I don't want a massacre, and, besides, we don't know how close Katherine will be to the action."

"Makes sense," Karl said. He grabbed a shortened shotgun and some boxes of bean bag rounds. "Oh, and some of these?"

He held up a pair of Tasers, and looked at Steve inquiringly.

"Why not?" Steve said.

While Karl was working out how the Tasers operated, Steve tried the phone again, not really expecting a different result—and not getting one. Ignoring Karl's questioning look, he walked over to a set of lockers that ran all the way along one of the walls. He rummaged around and brought out two pairs of thermal imaging scopes.

"Some of these, I think. And these."

He threw a bulletproof vest to Karl. It was a lighter model than anything available on the open market, and as Karl put it on, it molded to his frame perfectly.

"Better safe than sorry, right?"

"Anything that lessens my chances of catching a bullet is good by me," Karl said. "What have you got there, Steve? What is this, *Robin Hood*?"

Rogers was holding what looked like a squat, bulbous crossbow. Along the haft were a number of vicious looking bolts, all with an odd metal loop at the rear of their shafts.

"You'll see," Steve said. "I think we're almost done here. Anything else you can think of?"

Karl held up a bandolier of stun grenades. "Flash and bang."

"Good call," Steve said.

"So, um, Steve, is it okay if I take one of these?" Karl was holding the Colt. "I mean, if it's not cool . . ."

Steve laughed. "Go for it. I've already broken any number of regulations by bringing you here."

Steve grabbed a black duffel bag and loaded it with their selections. Pausing for a moment, he grabbed another vest and threw it in, and then added a set of transceivers. Karl helped, and when the bag was full, Steve picked it up, barely feeling the weight.

"You really are feeling better, aren't you?" Karl said. "How close are you to peak performance?"

Steve shrugged. "Eighty percent, maybe? It doesn't really matter, I have to be good enough for what we're about to do. Katherine needs us."

Karl was still stuffing his pockets with extra rounds and a number of magazines for his new toy. "Don't worry, those guys aren't going to know what hit them."

"I hope not. I hate hostage situations—there are too many variables, too many things that can go wrong."

"Yeah, I've been involved in my share. But that's the thing, I have the experience and the training to deal with exactly this scenario, and you . . . well, you're Captain America."

When Steve didn't return his grin, Karl frowned.

"What's wrong?"

Steve simply held up the phone, putting it on speaker and letting Karl hear it ring out.

"I've been trying to contact my source at S.H.I.E.L.D., Katherine's aunt, Maria," Steve said. "She isn't answering my calls and I'm starting to worry. It might just be that I'm using one of our burner phones and she doesn't want to take even the small risk it could be compromised. My phone was packed with all sorts of extra tech, and she knew the number, but it didn't survive the fight that laid me up. I hope that's it, anyway."

Steve tried not to think of the alternatives. He had to trust that Maria could look after herself—after all, she had certainly shown she could in the past.

"So, no cavalry?" Karl asked. "No one else you can contact?"

"I can't just get anyone involved. If anything, this is a

S.H.I.E.L.D. operation, so really I should be calling them for backup." Steve said. "The problem with that is I simply don't know who I can trust. Maria is the only one I can be sure of."

Karl shrugged. "If that's the way it is, then I guess it's up to us, Cap, and I'd back us any day," Karl said. "Like I said, we have unique talents that make us perfect for this. And we have one advantage that I never had on any of my past missions—something that would have made those extractions so much easier."

"What's that?" Steve asked.

"Katherine is no good to them dead. They need her research, and that means that they need her." He looked up at Steve. "That's our trump card."

Steve suddenly felt a whole lot better about things. He had been so caught up in his concern for Katherine that he had forgotten that simple truth.

"Thank you, Karl," he said. "I needed that."

Karl shrugged uncomfortably.

"It's no big deal, just spelling it out for you. Now, are we going to stand around here chatting, or are we going to go get Katherine back?"

Chapter 13

"**A**re you sure you're up to this?" Karl asked. "You still don't look like you're at your best."

"Oh, I'm fine," Steve said, with a confidence he didn't feel. "Just a bit sore. Once I get moving, I'll be as good as new."

They were prone on the roof of a tall building that overlooked the Four Seasons Hotel. They were up high enough that they could see down into the penthouse suite, which took up the entire top floor of the hotel. Steve had discarded his civilian clothes and was back in his uniform, shield strapped to his back. He felt much more comfortable—and ready for anything.

"For freedom fighters, these guys certainly live the high life, don't they?" Karl remarked. "So much for this 'every minute we wait is a minute my people are suffering' and all that."

Steve had to agree. He had nothing against enjoying the comforts of life when you could, but they had been watching the TLF for hours now through thermal imaging scopes, and had counted at least six room service deliveries.

"So, I've got eleven men." He swept the scopes back across the room one last time just to be sure. The walls may as well have not been there; the occupants of the penthouse showed up as crystal clear, if green-tinted, figures. Steve counted them off.

"One at each compass point, that's four. Two on patrol, that's six. One at the main door, that's seven. And four in the main rooms, that's eleven, plus a smaller image that I assume is Katherine. Is that what you have?"

"That's affirmative. Looks like the smaller figure is seated and restrained." Despite the neutral language, Steve could hear the anger simmering below Karl's words.

"When we go in, we go in hard and fast. But remember, emotion can't come into it," Steve said. "That's the only way we'll get her out."

"Don't worry, Captain. I've been here before."

Steve clapped him on the shoulder. "I know you have. Glad to have you on my side."

Steve got to his feet with barely a twinge. He really was getting better, but whether it was better enough was something they'd find out soon.

"Are you ready?" he asked Karl.

"No time like the present," Karl said. He gathered up his equipment, double checking that his shotgun was loaded with bean bag rounds. He hesitated, then slid his M1911A1 into the holster at his side.

"Remember, nonlethal rounds unless absolutely necessary, okay?" Steve said, noticing Karl's motion.

Karl nodded. "It's just some insurance, that's all. Absolute last resort."

Steve took the strange, hybrid crossbow and walked to the edge of the building. "So, when we get over there, you go left, I go right. We take out the men at the compass points, scooping up the patrols on the way, then meet at the main door and take out the sentry. Then we worry about the ones in the main area of the room."

"They'll know we're there by then, and they'll be waiting," Karl warned, even though they'd gone over the plan a half dozen times by then.

"I can't see anything we can do about that," Steve said. "We just have to hope you're right about Katherine's value to them."

"It's risky, but I don't see any other option. There's only two of us."

"Then we'll have to be twice as careful." Steve looked across the gap and nodded to himself. "Let's do it."

Steve raised the crossbow and sighted across the gap between the two buildings. He squeezed the trigger and, with a puff of compressed air, a bolt shot out, a line of cable unraveling behind it. The bolt hit the concrete above the balcony door, setting off a tiny charge in its shaft that drove metal spikes deep into the wall. Steve tugged on it and grunted with satisfaction—there wasn't any give, no matter how hard he yanked on it. He tied off the cable around a metal bar protruding from the rooftop and then walked over to the duffel bag.

"Here you go." He tossed a harness over to Karl, who looked at it, then at the cable.

"Are you sure that's going to hold our weight?" he asked doubtfully. "It looks awfully thin."

"It's a spider silk and steel composite," Steve said. "You could suspend a truck from it. I think you'll be okay."

Karl shrugged and put the harness on. Steve did the same, and then clipped them both to the cable.

"Here's the quick release. As soon as we hit the balcony, unclip, and go hard and fast."

With that, Steve kicked off the rooftop, his weight sending him hurtling across the gap between the two buildings. When he neared the Four Seasons, he hit the quick release and was already moving when his feet landed on the balcony. Using his momentum, Steve dove through the balcony windows, tucking himself into a forward roll. He hit the first of the men in a spray of wood and glass, sending him flying into the wall with a nasty crunch. Steve was already up by the time the other man had recovered enough to reach for his gun, and he sent him flying with an uppercut. He heard a crash and a stream of profanity behind him; Karl arriving, he assumed.

"Okay, let's go."

Rogers headed right, trusting Karl to do his job. As he rounded the corner, Steve came face to face with a guard armed with a shotgun. Rogers didn't even slow down, instead charging the TLF man, who only had time to get off a single round, buckshot screaming off Steve's shield in all directions. Rogers used his momentum to carry himself past the man, clipping him on the temple with the rim of the shield and sending him crumpling to the ground. He kept moving, listening for the sound of the patrol. There. The other two men came rushing around the corner, pistols already in hand. It did them no good; Steve was already on them. He dropped his shoulder and sent one of them flying, then kicked out, sending the other man's pistol spinning through the air. The TLF soldier was experienced enough to not waste time scrambling after his gun, and instead reached for his hip and pulled out a knife. Its edge gleamed wickedly as he came in low and fast, the knife heading straight toward Steve's stomach.

Steve brought the blade of his hand down on the other man's wrist, sending the knife flying. The other man again showed his experience by not letting the loss of another weapon distract him, and immediately brought his other hand around, driving his fist into Steve's side. The body armor absorbed most of the blow, and Steve brought up his elbow, driving it into the other man's solar plexus. As the man fell forward, Steve rapped him on the skull with the rim of his shield. That was another man down.

For the first time since he had entered the penthouse, Steve had a chance to look around. He'd made a mental diagram before launching the raid, but that hadn't prepared him for the sheer opulence of the place. It was built in a pattern of concentric squares, the big center square of the main living areas surrounded by a square hallway that ran the whole way around it. At each corner was another square that held a luxuriously appointed room with its own en suite. The decor was old world—leather and oak with gold fittings and meticulously replicated oil paintings of dead generals. Steve wondered how much a place like this cost, then gave up—it was too far outside his experience to even guess.

He kept moving around the hallway, thankful for the sloppiness of the TLF guards. Instead of standing right at the corner, where he could have seen all the way down the corridor in either direction, the next guard was lounging against the wall, smoking an evil-smelling cigarette. He didn't even have time to straighten up before Steve was on him; he was down in seconds. Steve considerately butted out the man's cigarette.

"I'm doing you a favor. Those things will kill you."

By the time he reached the main entrance, Karl was already there. The last of the guards had turned to deal with him, and it was a simple matter for Steve to come up behind the guard and catch him in a sleeper hold, Rogers' muscular arms compressing the man's blood vessels and cutting off the circulation to his brain. The man struggled in his grip, but to no avail, and was soon unconscious on the floor.

They'd been quiet, and the walls were thick, but Steve had to think that the men in the other room were aware of the intruders. He regretted letting the guard get off even one shot, knowing it might have been enough noise to give them away, but he wasn't sure what other option he'd had.

"So, what's the plan, Cap?" Karl whispered. "Are we going with the full frontal assault?"

"I have an idea," Steve replied.

He knelt down next to the unconscious man and shook him. When there was no response, he slapped the man across the face, forehand then backhand. The man groaned and stirred, weakly pawing at Steve's hands. He opened his eyes, only to flinch as he looked straight down the barrel of Karl's Colt.

"Hello, friend," Steve said conversationally. "I just wanted to thank you."

"Thank me?" the man said on confusion. "My English, I don't think you mean what I think?"

"Oh, I do. You're going to help us out. You just don't know it yet."

Steve hauled the man to his feet and spun him around.

"You were right, Karl. We needed that last resort."

Karl cocked his pistol and nodded.

"Ready?" Steve asked.

"Always," Karl said. "I'll cover the left—you take the right."

Steve pushed the man in front of him. "Knock on the door and tell them that you need to speak with your leader. Make sure you sound convincing—Karl here knows enough Temasikian to catch you if you try and give us away."

Steve didn't know if that was true, but the man took one look at Karl's expression and gulped, then nodded. Rogers pushed the man up to the door, and he rattled off a few sentences in Temasikian. Another voice replied from behind the door, eliciting a back-and-forth between the two. Finally, after what seemed to be an incredibly long time to Steve but which was probably only a few minutes, the door slowly opened. The second man's eyes widened as he took in the sight in front of him, but before he could react, Steve barreled his captive into the other man, sending him crashing to the floor.

Before the two men had even hit the ground, Steve and Karl were though the door, Rogers' shield ready and Karl's gun pointing at the TLF members in the room. Four of them stood in a semicircle with Katherine in the middle. She was seated, bound to her chair, and Ernst held his gun against her head. Her eyes were wide and frightened, staring at Steve over the gag that covered the bottom half of her face.

"Don't move or I will splatter her brains all over this room," Ernst said, venom dripping from his voice. "Drop your weapons."

"Before you do anything hasty, why don't you ask one of your men what's on your forehead right now?" Karl said.

Ernst looked baffled for a moment, then rattled off a question in Temasikian. One of the men replied in the same language, pointing at Karl and then at the red dot that sat in the middle of Ernst's forehead.

"I love this gun," Karl said. "I can blow your head off right now, and know within a millimeter where the bullet will enter your brain."

"That might be true, but can you be sure I won't get a shot off first?" Ernst asked. Despite himself, Steve had to admire the man's self-possession. He could have been discussing the weather for all the emotion in his voice.

"That's the only reason you're still alive," Karl said. "Steve may be one of the good guys, but I would have no compunction at all about putting a pill in you right here and now. Tell your men to put their weapons down on the ground."

Ernst gave him a venomous glare, then nodded to his men. They laid their weapons on the ground and kicked them over to Steve.

"Now what?" Ernst asked. "This is a standoff. You can't shoot me, and I can't shoot you."

"There is a big difference, though," Karl replied.

"And what's that?" Ernst asked.

"We don't need you alive," he said coldly. "But you need what's in Katherine's head. The only thing in your skull is something that, unless we get the girl back, has an appointment with my bullet in about five seconds."

Ernst laughed. "I think you overestimate her value. Yes, what she has will help our cause, maybe even be a turning point. But we have fought for decades without her, and we will fight on for decades more if need be."

"I don't believe you," Karl said uneasily.

"Believe this—I will sooner kill her than give her back. If we cannot have her research, then no one will." The mask had dropped fully now, and Steve could hear the fanaticism burning in the man's voice.

"You'll die, too," Karl said weakly.

"You think I am scared to die? I have been dead for eighteen years, since the moment I joined the struggle. It is only a matter of time." Ernst smiled a death's-head smile. "It may as well be here, among such comforts, as anywhere else. And if I take down Captain America with me, there will not be a person in the world who doesn't know of the TLF and our glorious struggle."

"You're insane," Karl said. "You want to die."

"No; if I can walk away from this, I will do so happily. I still have much to offer my people. I just wish to ensure you are under no illusions as to how much leverage you have in this situation. My willingness to negotiate has its limits."

"Then I guess we have a stalemate," Karl said. "It's okay, I can wait as long as you can."

"Do you have reinforcements coming?" Ernst asked abruptly. "Are you so confident they will be here soon?"

Karl hesitated. "Of course we do." It was too late; his pause had given them away.

"I thought as much. Time was of the essence for you. No time to arrange backup," Ernst said. "Well, I have been in this country for a few weeks now, and I have had my men in meetings all up and down the East Coast. This is our rendezvous point; we meet here before we leave for the airport. There's a half dozen of my soldiers on their way here as we speak."

"You're bluffing," Karl said.

"Why don't you just wait and see about that?" Ernst said. "They are meant to be here in five minutes, and my men are nothing if not punctual."

Steve and Karl looked at each other. Steve knew that the delicate balance that they had been able to create would not survive the introduction of more variables.

"What if I go with you?" Steve stepped forward, lowering his shield to rest at his side.

"What?!" Both Karl and Ernst said at the same time, then stopped and looked at each other suspiciously.

"What do you mean?" Ernst asked

"I'm not letting you take her, not by herself. Take me too, and that way I'll be assured of her well-being. I won't interfere at all—I'll just be there as her bodyguard."

"Are you crazy, Cap?" Karl nearly yelled. "You can't be seriously considering helping these . . . these maniacs."

"I promised I would keep Katherine safe, Karl, and I always keep my promises. I can't really see any other options right now, can you?"

Karl shook his head.

"How do we know we can trust you?" Ernst asked.

"Because I would give you my word that I wouldn't intervene as long as you treated Katherine with every courtesy," Steve said. "And in return, you would agree to release us after a set term, say three months—time enough for Katherine to show you how best to implement her research. That way, you get what you want, and I get what I want. Sound fair?"

For once, Steve felt little guilt at lying. He would back himself to find a way to free Katherine, given time and opportunity, but he needed to get her out from under their guns—and to do that he would need to sell them on his idea.

"Very fair. But hard for me to believe," Ernst said. "You would give in, just like that? Allow yourself to become a tool of our cause? Your pride would surely not allow such a thing."

"That's where you and I are different. Yes, I have my pride, but I would never sacrifice someone else to it. A little bit of pride is a good thing—we have to have that to function in this world, to keep our heads up when things get tough. But when it matters more to us than another person—well, that's when it becomes poison."

"Very noble, Mr. Rogers," Ernst said contemptuously. "But I think I will wait for my men to arrive and take my chances."

"Is that your final decision?" Steve asked. "Are you sure you don't want to reconsider before it's too late?"

"More threats? They grow wearisome."

"Not at all," Steve said. "Just when you leave someone with nothing to lose, you create a very volatile situation."

The sound of footsteps came from the hallway, and Ernst smiled nastily.

"It looks like you are out of time, Mr. Rogers."

Steve tensed, ready to lunge across the room and hopefully get to Ernst before his men arrived. But before he could move, there was a series of small explosions, sounding as if they were coming from all around them, and then gunfire and the sound of struggling.

"Rogers, call off your men or I will kill her right here and now, I swear!" Ernst yelled. His knuckles whitened as his finger tensed on the trigger.

"My men?" Steve asked. "I hope they're coming to help

us, but you have to believe I don't have any control over them. Hurting her won't stop them." He looked at his companion. "Karl?"

Karl shook his head wordlessly.

The surprise in Steve's voice must have convinced Ernst, and he barked orders to one of his men, who took his place covering Katherine. The other men took up positions to either side of Ernst, facing the door, guns drawn.

"If they aren't with you, and they aren't with me, then who are they?" he asked Steve.

"A lot of people want that research," Steve said. "It could be any of number of people."

"Whoever it is, they are going to regret this," Ernst said.

He and his men braced themselves. Steve and Karl were still deciding what to do when black-clad men burst thought the door and all hell broke loose.

Chapter 14

Four men in black body armor swarmed into the room, and the Temasikians dove for cover. Bullets shredded a very expensive leather couch that Ernst ducked behind. Steve dove too, but toward Katherine, knocking her chair over as he tried to get her out of the line of fire.

"Cease fire! Cease fire, you idiots!" A voice rang out from the doorway. "We're here for the girl."

The sound of gunfire cut off as if a switch had been flicked, and an eerie silence filled the room. It held for a moment, and then was broken by a shout from Ernst.

"Get the woman!"

Two TLF men darted across the room, and a pair of the black-clad men rushed to intercept them. As they traded blows, Ernst made a beeline for the door, but before he could make it, the doorway was filled by a squat figure. Steve recognized the man from the safe house even before he pulled the two short staves from the holsters on his back.

"You're not going anywhere," Jonah said.

Ernst stopped. "Are you going to try and stop me?"

"No, I'm not going to try." He twirled the staves in the hypnotic, blurring circles that Steve remembered from their last encounter.

As quick as a flash, Ernst grabbed one of the lamp stands and snapped off either end. This left him with a short staff, about five feet long, that he held with the practiced familiarity of a man who had used such a weapon before. He dropped into a fighting stance and waited for the other man to attack. Jonah swung his staves overhead, bringing them down on the staff with a wooden crack. As if that was merely the opening salvo, the two men shifted into another gear. Their weapons turned into blurs, and the sound of wood on wood filled the room with a syncopated tempo that would have done any self-respecting thrash drummer proud. Behind them, the other men were still fighting, the occasional smack of fists on flesh or anguished groan the only noise.

Steve didn't waste time staring at the deadly dance going on in the middle of the room or at the other distractions. He was already working on Katherine's bonds. The TLF hadn't made his job easy—it looked they had wrapped a whole roll of duct tape around her ankles, and another around her wrists.

"Here."

Karl passed him a clasp knife, and Steve sawed away at the tape while the other man watched his back. Trusting Karl, Steve didn't even look up when he heard a meaty thunk and one of the TLF members fell to the ground next to him. Finally, he had Katherine free and her hands went to her mouth and pulled out the gag.

"Thanks, but why leave the gag until last?" Katherine asked, spitting out bits of tape and fluff.

"Because I didn't want you telling me how to get rid of the rest?" He held up his hand. "Teasing! Are you okay?"

"Yeah, just sore and cramped from sitting in the same position for hours."

"They didn't hurt you?" Karl asked. His tone of voice made it clear that someone was going to be sorry if she said yes.

"No, Ernst made it very clear that they needed me in a fit state to help with their plans, and I think he was worried if he went too far, they would never be able to convince me to help."

"That's good," Karl said. "I was worried." He paused. "I mean, I know the research is important and all that."

Katherine gave him an appraising look, but before she could comment further, Steve interrupted.

"Hate to rush you or anything, but let's get out of here while we have the chance."

By then, Ernst was favoring his left arm and Jonah had a nasty bruise flowering above his eye. Both men were breathing heavily and their weapons were moving a touch slower than before, but even to Steve's trained eye, it was impossible to discern who was on top.

"Karl, deal with the others."

The former Marine nodded, raised his shotgun and, with chilling efficiency, turned and opened fire. The bean bags might not have been lethal, but they were effective, and in a matter of moments the six men were down, unconscious or struggling to breathe. He swung around and pointed the shotgun at Ernst and Jonah, who froze almost midmotion and dropped their hands to their sides. Before they could say a word, Karl pulled the trigger again. There was only a click, and he cursed. In a blur of motion, Jonah slammed his stave into Ernst's gut and then smashed him over the head, sending him to the floor where he lay motionless. It was the work of seconds, but that was all the time the ex-Marine needed, and there was a gun in Karl's hand and leveled at Jonah before he could get to his own side arm.

"Drop it!" Karl snapped. "You don't have a play here, you know that, so let's save some time."

Jonah slowly bent and placed his gun on the ground.

"Kick it over to me."

Wordlessly, Jonah complied, and Karl picked the gun up, checking the safety before shoving it into his belt.

"Now, go and stand facing the wall, hands behind your head. I want you sniffing the wallpaper."

When Jonah was in position, Karl patted him down carefully, making sure he didn't leave himself vulnerable to any sudden moves. He found another gun in a holster tucked into Jonah's sock, and a nasty looking knife with a knuckle-duster grip strapped to the small of his back.

"You can't escape from here," Jonah said. "I have men waiting at every entrance to the building, and a dozen more positioned around the perimeter. You won't make it a hundred feet before they pick you up, and I can't answer for your safety. She's safe, but the two of you have targets painted on you."

"We'll take our chances," Steve said. "On your knees."

When Jonah hesitated, Karl pushed the barrel of his gun into the small of the other man's back. "Really? Are we going to play these games?"

Jonah said a foul word and dropped to his knees.

Steve had just started to bind Jonah with the tape the TLF had used on Katherine when Karl broke in.

"Hang on, Cap," he said. "Allow me."

"Be my guest," Steve said, stepping back.

Karl grabbed Jonah and pulled him back up. He wrapped his arm around the other man's neck and held his gun against Jonah's ear. Karl marched Jonah over to the doorway and down the hall, stopping in front of the fire doors next to the elevator.

"We have your boss." Karl said. "Come out with your

hands up, and no one gets hurt." He winked back at Katherine. "I've always wanted to say that."

There was no answer.

"Tell them I'm not bluffing."

When Jonah stayed silent, Karl ground the gun into his ear.

"Come out," Jonah gasped, "and lay down your weapons."

The doors opened, revealing the three sullen looking men who'd been waiting inside. Their hands were raised, guns in the air. Steve relieved them of their weapons, and Karl gestured them into the bedroom with his gun.

"Down on the floor. Flat on your stomachs, hands behind your heads."

The men complied, stretching out on the lush carpet. Steve bound them hand and foot with the leftover tape, wrapping it around their ankles and wrists. Karl pushed Jonah toward Steve, and Rogers gave him the same treatment. Just to be safe, Steve bound Ernst and the unconscious TLF fighters, too.

"Who are you working for?" Steve demanded of Jonah. The other man remained silent, staring defiantly back at his captors.

"We don't have time for this, Cap," Karl said. "If the building is surrounded, we need to hurry up and get moving."

"You know you won't get far," Jonah said. "You can't run far enough, or fast enough, to get away from us."

"We'll see about that," Steve said. "All I know is you won't be doing much running. Or walking. I'd take you with us, but I'm sure you'd do everything you could to slow us down, and we don't have time for that."

Steve, Karl, and Katherine hurried into the corridor, scanning for further threats. The hallway was littered with bodies, mainly TLF members, but seasoned with a few of the black-clad men who had come with Jonah.

"Where to now?" Katherine asked. "You heard what he said—there are people surrounding the building."

"Watch and wonder," Karl said.

He led them into the elevator and fiddled with the panel.

"In most of these places, you have to have a room key to get to certain floors. It stops the wrong element from wandering around. But even a room key generally won't get you to the utility areas or the basement. However, a man with the right sort of skills can generally bypass that, and in the basement, there are all sorts of access tunnels. Some for freight, some for waste. It's . . ."

"It's a way out of here!" Katherine interrupted. "That's brilliant, Karl!"

Karl grinned. "Well, I can't help being a genius. It's a curse really."

A shower of sparks fell as Karl pulled his hand away, cursing. The smell of burning filled the elevator.

"Genius, huh?" Steve asked.

"It's not as bad as it looks," Karl said defensively. "And, look, here we go."

He was right—the number indicator flashed, showing that they were heading down. The three of them kept their eyes on the big letter *B*, and let out a cheer when it glowed. The doors slid open, revealing the cavernous hotel basement.

"Voilà," Karl said. "Did I deliver, or did I deliver?"

He held out his fist. "Don't leave me hanging, K."

Katherine grinned and bumped Karl's fist. "Just don't call me 'K,' okay?"

Steve was already in the basement, checking for threats. He stopped when he found a large steel grate.

"I think I've found what we're looking for," he yelled back to the others. "I just hope neither of you are scared of the dark."

"Do we have to?" Katherine said. "If you're suggesting what I think you're suggesting, I'd really rather not."

"I don't think we have a choice," Steve said. "It could be worse, trust me on that."

"What do you mean?" Karl asked.

"Never mind," Steve muttered.

Steve bent down and grabbed the grate. He braced himself, and with a grunt, lifted it out of place, dragging it to the side. He looked down into the hole. There was a glint of water, and the faint whiff of grease and sewage.

"Okay, this one is much worse." Steve turned to the others. "Karl, you go first, then I'll lower Katherine down."

"Man, why do I have to go first?" Karl said.

"Because you're the ex-Marine and Katherine is the computer tech. No offense, Katherine."

"None taken. I'm happy not to go first!"

"And you, Cap? I'm happy to let you go first."

"Can you pull the grate shut behind us? It weighs about six hundred pounds."

"You make a good point," Karl said. "Sorry, it's just . . . are there going to be rats down there, do you think?"

"Aw, is the big bad man scared of a teensy little rat?" Katherine teased.

"If you'd been captured by insurgents and watched them use rats as a form of torture, you might not be a fan either," he snapped.

Katherine's face fell. "I was just kidding, Karl. I'm sorry."

"Don't worry about it—I know you didn't mean anything by it." He turned back to the hole and peered down. "Okay, if I have to do this, let's get it over with."

He put a hand on either side of the drain and lowered himself down, trying to get as low as he could before he let go. He dropped, and Steve and Katherine heard a splash followed by the sound of Karl cursing.

"Oh man! It stinks down here. Like a mix of sweaty feet and moldy cheese. I think I'm gonna be sick."

Katherine was trying not to laugh, and Steve gave her a mock-severe look.

"I wouldn't say too much; you're next."

She sighed and walked over to edge of the hole.

"I really don't like the look of this."

Steve ignored her. "Karl, get ready to grab her on the way down, okay?"

"Sure, Cap."

Rogers extended his hand and Katherine took it. He lowered her down into the drain, slowly, until he felt Karl take her weight.

"I've got her," Karl yelled from the drain.

Steve let Katherine go and stepped back.

"Move a few yards away, okay?" he yelled down. "Let me know when it's clear."

"Clear!"

Steve dragged the grate partially over the hole, then lowered himself in. He hung from the grate, swinging and using his body weight to shift it, feeling a jolt as it dropped back into place. He hung for a moment, and then dropped down, bending his knees as he landed. There was a splash of fetid water and a foul smell, but the footing was firm enough, and he walked over to where the other two waited.

"If this is below the basement of the hotel, we're well under street level. But, I think if we follow it, we'll either come to a way up, or cross over to another tunnel. We can make a decision when we get to that point, but I want us at least few blocks away before we even surface to check out our location. Sound like a plan?"

The other two nodded, and they set off. As they got farther away from the hotel, the smell diminished; Steve supposed that the hotel had been illegally dumping kitchen grease and waste into what was meant to be a storm-water drain. As the water cleared, their surroundings became a lot more bearable and—much to Karl's loud and expressive relief—aside from a few squeaking and scuttling noises that came from the smaller side tunnels, there was no sign of rats. Every so often, the darkness was broken by a beam of sunlight shining down a ventilation shaft, giving them a break from the oppressive blackness.

To start with, they tried talking among themselves, but the way that their voices echoed back brokenly from the drain's walls made it sound as if there were people following them, or even in front of them, and the eerie noises saw even Katherine soon give up on trying to keep the conversation going. Once they stopped talking, the dead silence that enveloped them made Steve think that they had been imagining it.

They walked in silence for almost an hour before Steve decided it was worth checking out where they were. The next access ladder they came to was rusted and broken, so they kept going until they found one that looked capable of bearing their weight.

"Wait here," Steve said. "I'll make sure the coast is clear. No point in all of us getting caught."

He climbed the ladder, testing each rung carefully as he went. He was only just starting to feel like his old self again, so the last thing he needed was to fall back down into a storm drain. It didn't take him long to reach the surface, and he carefully eased the manhole cover out of the way. He peeked over the rim and recoiled at the sight of a gun barrel pointed straight at his face. He pushed himself back off the ladder and let himself fall, landing with a splash of water and stumbling slightly in the muck. Steadying himself, he looked up, then froze. Karl and Katherine were kneeling in the shallow water, their hands behind their heads. A familiar figure stepped out from the circle of gunmen who had weapons trained on Steve's companions, chuckling as he sneered at Steve.

"I told you we were watching *all* of the exits," Jonah said. "My men were good enough to wait until I was free to bring you in."

Steve looked around, searching for a way out. He didn't like what he saw—the sewer was blocked at both ends by Jonah's men, and they couldn't risk a firefight in such enclosed quarters. There was no cover at all, and they were exposed to a superior force. Resistance would have been suicidal.

"I have to hand it to you, Jonah—I think you've got the upper hand right now."

"You don't say."

"So, what happens now?"

Jonah looked around. "Well, first of all, we take you somewhere more pleasant and have a little conversation. When I say pleasant, I mean the surroundings—I doubt that any of you are going to enjoy the conversation too much."

He gestured to two of the men and they grabbed Steve, taking one arm each and pinning them behind him. Conscious of the guns trained on him and his companions, he didn't struggle, even when Jonah came close enough to grab.

"But, first, I think I owe you a little something."

His eyes did not betray his intentions, but Steve suspected what was coming. He'd already tensed his muscles when Jonah drove a fist into his stomach with a jab that had no wind up at all, all the power coming from the flexion of his hips. Even ready for it, Steve grunted in pain—the man could hit—and hunched around the blow. He straightened just in time to see the stock of Jonah's gun coming straight for his head, and then everything went black.

Chapter 15

Steve was sick of waking up in strange beds. His chin ached, but other than that, he seemed fine. He searched his memory, trying to remember how he had come to be in this situation—and then it all came rushing back. He sat up, or at least tried to, straining against his restraints until the frame of the bed creaked in protest. But there was no give in them at all and, after a few minutes of vein-popping, sweat-inducing effort, he slumped back in the bed. With what range of movement he had, he scanned the room, looking for signs of his friends. They were nowhere to be seen, but there were two very large black-clad men standing on either side of the gleaming metal door, watching his efforts with emotionless faces.

"Enjoying the show?" he asked.

There was no response, not that he had expected one. He kept testing his bonds—it gave him something to do while he waited for whatever came next. His patience wasn't stretched too far, and only an hour or so passed before the light over the door changed from red to green. The two men snapped to attention as the door slid open and Jonah strode in, carrying Steve's shield. He walked over to the bed and looked down at Steve for a moment, then turned and walked back to the door. As he passed the sentries, he snapped out a command.

"Bring him."

The two men drew their side arms and came over to the bed. Steve was flattered by their caution—they made a point of only unfastening one arm at a time, with one of them remaining out of reach with his pistol pointed directly between Steve's eyes. Rogers sat up and his arms were manacled behind him, and only then was he dragged to his feet. Taking an arm each, the two men marched him after Jonah, their free hands holding their guns in readiness.

The room in which he had awoken was only one of many on that floor, and as they walked him through, he began to get an idea of the scale of the place. The elevator ride took several minutes, and they must have climbed at least a dozen floors before the doors opened and they stepped out.

Despite himself, Steve was impressed. The control center—for that's what it must have been—would not have been out of place at S.H.I.E.L.D. It was a cavernous space filled with desks, and at each one a technician worked at a computer. Covering the far wall, which was at least fifty feet tall, were a score of massive screens. As Steve watched, the images flickered and changed, scrolling through news channels from around the world or displaying satellite imagery from every major city Steve could imagine—and some he'd never heard of. Sentries stood guard at regularly spaced intervals around the room, and there was a constant hum of activity, men and women bustling back and forth.

He didn't have a chance to get much more of a look, as his captors didn't stop. Instead, they marched Steve around the perimeter, obviously avoiding taking him too close to any of the workers, and down a flight of stairs. It wound down for what must have been several stories until, at the bottom of the staircase, they came to a hallway with rows of identical doors on either side, differentiated only by the number that adorned each one.

"Number four is empty, boss," one of the men said.

"Good, take him in there, restrain him, and leave him."

"You sure that you want to handle this alone, boss?" the other man said, sounding doubtful.

"You don't think I'm capable of managing things myself?" Jonah asked.

"Of course not, boss," the other man said hurriedly.

They dragged Steve into room number four. The only furniture was a desk with a chair on either side, and they sat Steve down in one of the chairs. He could see his reflection in the mirror that took up the whole of the other wall, his face brought into sharp relief by the glare of the lamp shining directly into his eyes. He would have bet good money that there was a camera, if not a room for observers, on the other side of the glass. He'd been in so many interrogation rooms that he had lost count, and there were common elements that they all seemed to share. At least this one was clean and modern, not hewn out of a cave somewhere.

Pipes were welded on either side of the chair, obviously for the express purpose of keeping people restrained. The two men took advantage of this useful addition, making sure Steve wasn't going anywhere before they left. Jonah stood, watching Steve for a moment, and rapping his knuckles on Steve's shield before hanging it on the wall and taking the seat across from Rogers. He simply sat for moment, not saying a word as he waited for the door to close behind the exiting men. When they were finally alone, he spoke.

"Do you consider yourself a patriot, Rogers?"

It certainly wasn't what Steve was expecting Jonah to open with.

"I'd like to think so," Steve replied carefully. "Kind of goes with the name."

"Anyone can call themselves a patriot or wear a badge— or carry a shield like you do—but do you love this country?"

"No one can question my love for this country. I've sacrificed more than you can imagine, and I would give my life in its service." Steve was angry now. "Who are you to question me?"

Jonah gave him another appraising look, seemingly

searching for something in Steve's expression. Whatever it was, he must have found it. With the air of a man who had made a difficult decision, he leaned forward.

"That's what I've heard. And I believe it. That's why we're having this conversation. I think, given the opportunity, you'll do the right thing and there won't be any need for any more . . . unpleasantness."

"Unpleasantness? Is that what we're calling it? Forgive me if I'm not in any mood to make things easier for you."

"All I'm asking is for a conversation."

"You want to talk? Okay, then tell me something, Jonah—this is an impressive facility. Big money behind it. Who are you really working for? Hydra?"

Jonah laughed. "You really are on the wrong track, Rogers. You couldn't be further from the truth."

"Then who? Where did you go after S.H.I.E.L.D.? Some international crime syndicate? A foreign power?"

"Getting colder. Rogers, you need to understand I'm a patriot, too. Maybe not as long standing as you, but I like to think that my love for this nation is just as fervent. I'm still working for the United States government. Just for a different agency."

"And which agency is that?" Steve asked skeptically. "It's none of the usual suspects, otherwise it wouldn't be such a mystery as to where you ended up. Word gets around, you know."

Jonah sat back in his chair.

"As I said, I believe you're a patriot. More importantly, a lot of very influential people agree. We wouldn't be having this conversation otherwise. There are only three people who can grant clearance for the information I'm about share with you, and at least one of them is a fan of yours."

"What knowledge? Will you stop dancing around and just tell me?"

Jonah looked a little chagrined, as if Steve were ruining his fun by cutting to the chase.

"The agency I work for has a very specific role in keeping the secrets of the United States government. You might say that's the job of any of the intelligence agencies, but our focus is different. We don't concern ourselves with keeping secrets from foreign powers or criminal elements."

"What do you mean?"

"Consider us glorified cleaners. Our job is to clean up the messes that would embarrass the government and ensure that secrets that the average citizen doesn't need to know—or isn't able to handle—remain just that. Secret. We get sent in when something happens and it's vital to national security that the truth never gets out."

"I've been in this business long enough to know that most things have a way of getting out," Steve said. "Even if it is just interagency chatter."

"Not with us, they don't. Otherwise, you would have

known where it was that I went after S.H.I.E.L.D." Jonah gave a rueful chuckle. "All these so-called secret organizations, but the thing is—if people know their names, they can't be that secret, right?"

"If it's so secret, then why are you telling me?"

"Because I need your help. And I believe that when you know what's at stake, you will help us—gladly."

"I honestly doubt that," Steve said. "Your methods haven't exactly filled me with confidence."

"Just listen to me, Rogers. This is too important to get all squeamish; what we do is so vital," Jonah said. "Part of governing is deciding what the people need to know, what they can handle. That's decided at a far higher level than you and me, but we're the ones tasked with implementing those judgment calls."

Steve shook his head. "Seems like we have very different ideas of good governance. I don't think that keeping things from the public is good policy."

"You say that, but would you want to see mass panics? People killed in riots? The government overthrown? You're looking at me like I'm crazy, but you have no idea of the catastrophes the people I work for have prevented."

"Then tell me," Steve said. "Educate me, Jonah."

"Where to start? Everyone has heard about Roswell, a nice little distraction we cooked up, but no one knows about the strange events in 1953, and the Skrull incursion in Salt

Lake City. Or how close we came to a mutant strain of Ebola killing everyone on the East Coast, which probably would have ended up having a mortality rate of 90 percent worldwide. Wrap your head around that number, Rogers. Imagine what would happen if that little tidbit had become public knowledge. There would have been mass panic, looting, a complete breakdown of order."

Jonah ran his hands through his short-cropped hair, and Steve noticed with surprise that he was shaking.

"Rogers, there's a never-ending list of these things. I wish that I didn't know about them all myself. You don't even want to know who was really on the grassy knoll, or what it would have meant if the world had learned the truth. All these pivotal moments in United States history, we were there, and because of us, no one knows what really happened."

"You realize you sound completely insane, right?" Steve asked. "There are whole TV channels of people talking like this."

"That's good. That's one of the tools we use when we have to cover something up. Portray anyone who's trying to spread the truth as crazy. There's enough of them out there, what's one more person wearing a tinfoil hat?"

"So, you're protecting people by lying to them, or making them think they're crazy?" Steve asked. "Not really my idea of what my government should be working toward. Then again, I have no proof that you have any real government sanction. You wouldn't be the only secret group running around the world with overinflated ideas of its own purpose."

Jonah didn't react to the scorn in Steve's voice. "I understand your skepticism, I really do."

Jonah pulled a mobile phone out of his pocket and placed it on the table, pushing it toward Steve. Steve looked at it, and then at Jonah.

"Really?" Steve asked. "You don't see the problem here?"

"Oh, right. Hang on."

Jonah walked around the table and unfastened one of Steve's hands, making sure he kept a prudent distance. He walked back around to his chair and took a seat.

"Dial the number on the screen."

Steve picked up the phone and dialed it. It rang twice before the call was picked up, and at the sound of the unmistakable voice that answered, he nearly dropped the phone in surprise.

"This is Secretary of State Ross speaking." The voice had the tone of someone used to giving orders. "Who's this, and how did you get this number?"

"Sir?" Steve frowned. He'd had no idea who he was calling, but General Thaddeus E. Ross would have been close to his last guess. "It's Captain Steve Rogers. I'm being held by a man who claims to represent the United States government."

There was a brief pause, the silence so complete Steve wondered if he'd been disconnected.

"His name?"

"Jonah."

"Describe him to me."

Steve gave an accurate, if not flattering, description of Jonah, and the general let out a deep breath.

"Captain, this man is who he says he is, and you can believe everything he claims, no matter how mad it sounds," Ross said.

"But, sir—"

"Captain, I'm not in the mood for arguing," Ross snapped.

"Sir, how do I know who I'm really talking to?" Steve said. "It's easier to believe that this is a very good impersonator than some of the crazy things I've just heard."

"That's fair enough, I suppose," Ross said grudgingly. "Ask me something only I would know."

Steve racked his brain for a moment, then it came to him.

"Apologies, sir, but what did Tony call you after the Guatemala mission two years ago?" Steve asked. "I hate to bring it up again, but only the three of us were there."

After a moment's silence, Ross ground out the word and Steve winced. He to admit, Stark had a way with words.

"Okay, sir, I accept this is you, thank you."

"Then, Captain, you need to accept my authority. The

man you are with represents the United States government and should be treated with the respect he is due as such. Do you need to be reminded of the oath you swore?"

"No, sir," Steve said. "But, I will ask you this question; is this man operating under your orders?"

"No, he is not part of my portfolio."

"Then whose authority is he under, sir? Can you tell me that?"

"No," Ross said "I can't. It's need to know only, and there are very few people who need to know. You are most definitely not one of them."

There was a click, and then silence. Steve pushed the phone back to Jonah, who walked around the table and resecured Steve's free hand.

"Well, you certainly have some high-level connections, I'll give you that," Steve said. He kept his voice level, but he was now very concerned. Steve had never really liked "Thunderbolt" Ross all that much. He'd always struck Steve as one of those officers who only knew one way to command—through harsh, unbending discipline with no room for compassion or mercy. But no one could have ever called the old man a coward, which was why the hint of fear in his voice was so unsettling.

He looked up at Jonah. "So what is this agency of yours called?"

"That name is a secret in itself," Jonah replied.

Steve shrugged. "Trust works both ways, you know. If you expect me to trust you . . ."

"That's true. Well, as you probably know by now, the government has a habit of changing agency's names from time to time, but we have always been known as Ex Umbra."

"From the shadows," Steve said, exercising his very rusty Latin.

"That's right, Rogers, well done. An apt name, given the necessity of staying out of sight. In fact, to ensure we are best placed to fulfill our mission, we have spent decades infiltrating as many other government agencies as we can, working from the concealment that they provide. We are very patient, and this process is helped by the fact that our members are all patriots and happy to serve the nation in any way they can. They act like any other employee of the agency they are part of, often better—working hard and moving up the ladder. You'd be surprised how much good they do, how much more effective they've made our government. They often end up in high-level roles, giving us more influence than you could imagine, which comes in very useful when we need to act. But their main purpose is to keep an eye out for secrets that we may have to step in to protect one day—and discover any threats to our ability to do so."

"So, Katherine's superiors—your men?" Steve asked.

"I don't see the harm in admitting that now," Jonah said.

"S.H.I.E.L.D. had always been a challenge for us, and for a long time Ex Umbra struggled to penetrate its defenses. That's nothing for S.H.I.E.L.D. to be proud of—it was because they had already been compromised by Hydra. After the clean out, it became slightly easier, but one of the reasons I was headhunted so aggressively was for the knowledge I would bring with me. I'd always thought S.H.I.E.L.D. was too soft, too willing to compromise, and once I was shown what Ex Umbra had done for this country, and was continuing to do, I was their man. I'm one of the lucky few, someone who has found their true calling."

"And like any convert, you wanted to spread the faith."

"Only to those who share our vision," Jonah said. "We use mercenaries from time to time, but all our agents believe in what we do as much as I do. I was able to use my knowledge of S.H.I.E.L.D. to recruit a select few I knew would be receptive to our work and who were already in place. It was fortunate that I did, or Katherine's research might have fallen into the wrong hands."

"Again, I have to ask, why are you telling me so much?" Steve asked. "What do you—what does Ex Umbra—want from me, exactly?"

"Isn't it obvious?" Jonah asked. "We need you to convince Katherine to hand over her research, destroy any copies, and sign an agreement that she will never share her research with anyone."

"But why? What is it about her research that scares you so much that you would go to such lengths to capture her?"

"Because if it does what she claims, then what secrets are safe? We can't afford to put a tool that powerful in the hands of the general populace. How could we put an embargo on updates coming from a situation we'd been called in to sanitize? That's the first thing we do when we move in. Her research is important enough that I will do anything to get it into our hands, even share our secrets with you and ask for your help."

"I don't know whether I can convince her to hand it all over to you," Steve said. "In fact, I don't even know whether I should try."

"I thought you said you were a patriot, Rogers?"

"I am. I just don't know if this falls under that umbrella. I've always believed that the American people are better than we often give them credit for being. What gives you the right to decide what they can or cannot know?"

Jonah scowled.

"The only reason that I stuck my neck out and told you all this was because I hoped you'd understand that sometimes this country needs to be protected from itself."

Steve matched him stare for stare. "I've found it more often needs protecting from those who think they know what is best for it."

"I can see that I misjudged you, Rogers," Jonah said.

"Forgive me if I find that more reassuring than anything else."

Jonah pulled out his phone and tapped a message. He gave Steve a long and considering look, then hit send.

"I didn't want to have to take this approach, but I guess I have no choice. We will get that information from Katherine, one way or another. And, as much as we would love to get our hands on the technology to work out countermeasures, ultimately our main concern is that no one else gets it, and there is a very simple solution to that particular problem."

For a moment, it was all Steve could do not to injure himself trying to break free of his restraints so he could leap across the table and throttle the other man.

"That won't help with the backup copy she put aside against any such eventuality," Steve said. He had no idea if Katherine had done that, but it seemed like the logical thing to do, and Katherine was nothing if not smart. "You know, the sort of thing that gets released if you die—or mysteriously disappear."

Jonah went pale as the blood drained from his face.

"You're bluffing."

"Am I?" Steve said mockingly. "From what you've told me, it would be a pretty big gamble on your part to call me on it."

"I guess that is another piece of information we will need to extract, one way or another."

"I know I'm old fashioned, but it seems to me that any country whose well-being requires you to threaten to torture a young woman is in deep, deep trouble."

"I will do whatever it takes to serve my country," Jonah said. "You can be as self-righteous about it as you want. I don't answer to you."

"Whatever it takes, Jonah? There has to be some measure of what is too far, or what are we fighting for?" Steve asked. "Who *do* you answer to, Jonah?"

"That's a state secret that you are not cleared for at this point, Captain."

"More secrets? That's the problem here, Jonah," Steve said. "When there are so many secrets, how can there be accountability?"

Jonah flushed.

"As much as I would love to sit here and discuss morality with you, I have other things to do with my time. You're a relic, Rogers, and you're clinging to values that have no place in the real world. While you congratulate yourself on how virtuous you are, I'll be in the trenches getting my hands dirty preserving this nation."

"Whatever helps you sleep at night, Jonah."

"I'm going to give you one last chance, Rogers. Have a think about what I've said, and decide what is more important—your country or that girl. When I come back, you'll need to make a decision. Either persuade her to give us her research, and the location of any backups, or I will. One way or another, by the end of today we will either have that knowledge, or we will have made sure no one else ever will. Am I clear?"

"Crystal," Steve said. "And while we're being so forthcoming, answer me something. Were you responsible for the attempts on her life?"

Jonah didn't flinch.

"Yes. I have full discretionary powers when on a mission, and I don't feel a need to pass the hard choices on to someone else. At that point, we still had her research on site, and we would have cracked her encryption eventually. And we had no reason to believe she had made any copies."

Jonah's gaze didn't waver as he looked Steve directly in the eyes, and Rogers realized he was in the presence of a true believer, a fanatic completely convinced of the rightness of his cause.

"I decided that the best option was to eliminate her. That way, we would ensure that her research wasn't further disseminated, and that control of such a powerful tool remained in more trustworthy hands. We didn't realize quite how complex the technology is, and that without her, may take years to fully understand."

"That was your best option?" Steve asked. "Attempted murder?"

"Is it murder when you shoot an enemy soldier?" Jonah

asked. "Never mind, it doesn't matter what either of us think. I was just following my orders to their ultimate conclusion."

"Even in my day, that was never a good enough excuse, Jonah. And I hear that there was a trial where they made that official—you might be familiar with it."

Jonah didn't respond, but simply stood and walked to the exit. It was only just as he was about to step through the door that he turned back to Steve.

"You have one hour. When I come back, you'll need to decide whose side you're on—and how we get what we need from Katherine."

Chapter 16

EX UMBRA HEADQUARTERS: 1400 HOURS

After Jonah left, Steve spent a fruitless thirty minutes trying to escape, rubbing his wrists raw against his restraints. No matter how much he struggled, there was no give in them, and eventually he simply settled back to wait. He was a seasoned enough campaigner to understand the importance of conserving energy for when it could actually do something. He resolved to bide his time and wait for the inevitable opportunity to present itself—and when it did, he would be ready seize it.

Steve took the silence as a chance to re-center himself, calling on some of the meditation techniques he had picked up over the years. He put aside the troubling revelations and his fears for Katherine, and focused on clearing his mind. By the time the light over the door flashed and Jonah walked back in, Steve was in a state of perfect calm.

Jonah stalked over and sat heavily in the chair across from Rogers. He stared at Steve, as if trying to force him to speak first, but Rogers merely regarded him with a placid expression. Finally, Jonah cracked.

"So, what's your decision?" he demanded. "Are you going to help us? Whose side are you on?"

"Freedom's," Steve replied evenly.

Jonah slammed his fists down on the desktop in frustration.

"What does that even mean?" he snarled. "The freedom to compromise your nation's security?"

"No, the freedom to live your life not worrying that your own government will try and have you killed, or hound you, or torture you. That's the freedom I've always stood for, that I believe this nation has always stood for. I think you've forgotten that somewhere along the line."

"Platitudes. Empty platitudes," Jonah spat. "Well, I gave you your chance. Let's see how you enjoy your freedom to choose when you see what it will cost you."

Jonah pressed the transceiver in his ear and murmured a few words. Mere minutes later, the doors slid open and two guards marched in. It was hard to tell if they were the same men from before—they were all cut from the same mold: big, brawny, and expressionless. They unfastened Steve from his chair and cuffed his hands behind his back, all while ensuring that he never had a clear shot at either of them or was not out of the firing line of one of their guns. As soon as they nodded to Jonah to signal they were done, he walked out the door, the two men dragging Steve along in his wake. They didn't have far to go, just to another door in the same hallway. From the outside, it looked identical to the one they had just come from, but when Jonah opened the door, it revealed a much bigger room.

In the middle was a circle of chairs facing inward, about ten feet from one side to the other. Katherine and Karl were both strapped in chairs directly opposite each other. The guards took Steve to a chair approximately halfway along the arc between the other two captives and sat him down. They stripped off his jacket and shirt, leaving him as bare chested as Karl was, then strapped him in. Once they were satisfied Steve couldn't move, they retreated to the entrance, taking positions on either side of the door. Jonah came and stood directly behind Karl, who was unable to turn his head far enough to keep the other man in sight. It was a classic power play that would leave Karl uneasy, his body telling him there was someone right behind him and that he had to do something—now. Steve had been on both sides of the equation, and he was painfully aware of how Karl would be feeling—and of exactly the advantage Jonah possessed.

"So, I'd hoped to avoid this sort of unpleasantness, but Mr. Rogers is refusing to cooperate," Jonah said. He looked over at Steve. "Last chance. Are you sure won't assist us with this?"

Steve shook his head. "I keep telling you, I don't think I

could persuade Katherine to do anything she didn't want to, even if I wanted to, which I don't. It's her research, her choice what she does with it."

Katherine shot him a grateful look, and then glared at Jonah.

"You tried to get Steve to convince me to give you what you wanted?"

"I made the error of thinking he was a patriot," Jonah said. "It seems I was mistaken."

"You were mistaken, all right," Karl said. "Steve and you have nothing in common. You talk about serving your country, but you wouldn't know the first thing about it. When I was on active service, we had words for people like you. I'm just too polite to say them in mixed company."

Jonah's hand tightened convulsively on the back of Karl's chair, knuckles going white, but Jonah's face remained expressionless.

"Thank you, you've just made my decision of where to start a whole lot easier." He pulled a black, rectangular object from his belt. It was about the size of two cigarette packets stuck end to end, with two copper projections at one end. Jonah pressed a button on the side and a row of five green LEDs lit up. "You've probably seen something like this before. You'd call it a Taser, though that's not strictly accurate—that's like calling just any photocopier a Xerox. It's a handy little device for dealing with people who are causing you problems when you don't want to do anything too . . . final."

Jonah pressed another button and a crackling blue bar of electricity arced between the two electrodes.

"That's fifty thousand volts of electricity right there. This one isn't a ranged weapon—some of them fire darts connected by wire filaments—this is a strictly an up close and personal version." He grinned. "Just the way I like it."

He triggered the electricity again, staring at the arc as if mesmerized.

"Besides, for our purposes, range is not really an issue." He looked at Katherine. "Last chance. Are you sure that you won't cooperate? I want the location of any backups and the names of anyone else you've told about this. Don't make this any worse than it has to be."

Katherine was pale, two spots of color burning on her cheeks, hands trembling where she clutched the side of the chair. But her voice was even when she replied, and Steve felt a rush of pride at her courage.

"No. This thing is bigger than me. And, I'm sorry, Karl, Steve, it's bigger than either of you."

Jonah shrugged. "Have it your way. Let's see how long your noble sentiments last."

He pressed the Taser against the metal frame of Karl's chair and pushed the button. There was a crackling noise and Karl went completely rigid, veins standing out on the side his neck. He moaned, a terrible, low groaning sound that made the hairs on Steve's arms stand up. Jonah kept the current flowing for less than fifteen seconds, but to Steve it seemed like an eternity. He couldn't imagine how long it must have seemed for Karl. When Jonah stopped, the ex-Marine slumped in his chair for a second, then straightened up.

"That . . . tickled," he said hoarsely. "Kind of warm and fuzzy. Like a kitten."

"Very brave," Jonah said. He looked over at Katherine. Her face was ashen and tears trickled out of the corners of her eyes. "I've been doing this for a long time, and I'm very good at it. In that time, I've learned something very interesting. You can inflict physical pain on someone and be surprised by how much they can take, but the same person will break within minutes if they're forced to watch someone else being tortured. Human beings are the most fascinating creatures, aren't they?"

"Katherine," Karl gasped. "Don't listen to him. Don't worry about me. You were right, this is bigger than both of us."

He convulsed as Jonah sent another wave of electricity running through him. This time, Jonah kept it running for thirty seconds; it took Karl longer this time to recover enough to talk.

"Is that all you've got? Seriously, man, I got worse than

that in hazing," he said slowly. "Maybe you need to check the batteries or something."

Jonah sighed. "I'll ask again, Katherine. Will you cooperate?"

She shot an anguished look at Karl, who shook his head.

"Don't . . . you . . . do . . . it," he ground out. "If I can handle this, you can handle watching."

"As you wish," Jonah said.

This time it seemed to go on and on. Steve could hear Katherine's stifled sobs over the sound of the arcing electricity and Karl's gut-wrenching moans.

"I can keep this up all day," Jonah said. "I'm not sure he can."

"Steve, what do I do?" Katherine pleaded. "I can't just watch this. I can't."

"I know it's hard, Katherine, but Karl and I made our choices, too. We're here because we believe in this cause, because we believe in you."

"That's easy for you to say!" she said, sobbing. "You're not the one suffering right now."

Steve gave her a sad smile.

"Oh, it'll be my turn next. Karl and I, we're the expendable ones. Jonah can't afford to damage that genius brain of yours."

At a strange drumming noise Steve whipped his head around. Karl's heels were hammering on the floor and his head was thrown back. A mix of foam and blood trickled from the corners of his mouth.

"What's happening to him?" Katherine screamed. "Do something!"

"He's having a seizure," Steve said.

Jonah stepped away from Karl and watched him impassively.

"That's right. It's only a minor one; he should be fine in a few minutes." Jonah seemed bemused. "Of course, too much more current and . . . well, he won't bounce back quite as quickly, if at all."

Karl had stopped shuddering and was slumped in the chair, the restraints the only things keeping him from sliding to the floor. Saliva ran down his chin and his eyes were vacant. Slowly, he came back to himself, straightening slightly. He groaned and tried to speak, but gave up and sat silently, taking deep, hitching breaths. Jonah moved back toward him, raising the Taser.

Steve could see that Katherine was about to crack.

"Jonah, if you kill him then that's one less piece of leverage you have. Don't be stupid, man."

Jonah gave Steve an appraising look.

"You make a good point," he said. "Perhaps I should give Karl here a break, let him recover a little before we start again. Of course, I'm too busy to stand around doing nothing. Lucky I have someone else here to take his place."

"Lucky," Steve muttered.

"Steve, I don't think I can do this," Katherine said. "I don't think I can keep watching."

"Yes, you can!" Steve said harshly. "I don't care what you have to do, close your eyes, think of a happy place, whatever gets you through it. Katherine, I know how brave you are. You aren't the weak link here."

By now, Jonah was behind Steve, who was very aware of the presence at his back. The skin on the back of his neck crawled, and he braced himself, waiting for the pain.

"I have this theory," Jonah said. "I've read your file, Rogers. You're not a superhuman, but you're enhanced, right? Speed, strength, stamina—all at the absolute top end of human performance. If you were crooked and no one knew who you were, you could win gold medals in any sport you chose, or have more Super Bowl rings than you've got fingers."

"Is there a point to this, Jonah?" Steve asked. "Or do you just like the sound of your own voice?"

"Oh, I have a point. A question to be precise. Did all those enhancements affect your nervous system? I mean, you have those reflexes, so that would suggest so. Does that mean that you feel more strongly than you did before? Because if so," he paused, "this is really going to hurt."

He pressed the Taser against Steve's bare shoulder and pushed the button. Agony lanced through Steve, fire burning along every nerve. His muscles contracted and pain stabbed into every pore. Coherent thought fragmented, shattering on the unyielding sensation of the electricity pouring through him, and time lost any meaning. Finally, thankfully, it stopped, but Steve kept shuddering even after Jonah had pulled the Taser away.

"I guess that answered my question," Jonah said. "I had another theory. Want to hear it?"

"You're full of ideas today, aren't you?" Steve gasped. "It's like watching *MythBusters*."

Jonah ignored Steve's weak attempt at humor.

"I'm willing to bet that your body can take a lot more punishment than Karl's before those brain cells start to short circuit," Jonah said. "That means more pain with less permanent damage, which makes this a lot easier for me."

"You've got all this figured out, haven't you?"

"Not really," Jonah said. "I'm just spitballing here. I could be really wrong. The upside for me is that if I am wrong, I won't be the one who ends up with brain damage."

This time the pain went on so long that even Steve's extraordinary constitution was pushed too far. Black bloomed before his eyes, and a rushing filled his ears before he blacked out. When he came to, Jonah was snapping his fingers in front of his eyes. Katherine sobbed in the background.

"Still with us, Rogers?" Jonah asked him. "Or was I wrong, and is that brain completely fried?"

"You'll have to do better than that," Steve said.

He didn't really believe his words; he wasn't sure how much more he could take, but he knew that he had to keep up a brave front for Katherine's sake. If she gave up the backups, she was as good as dead; it was merely a matter of time. The knowledge that Ex Umbra still needed was the only weapon she had left—once they had enough of her research to satisfy them, she was a loose end waiting to be tied off. Nothing he had seen or heard of Ex Umbra so far had led him to believe that they would hesitate for a single second.

"Okay," Jonah said. "Happy to oblige."

The pain burned through Steve. He gritted his teeth, trying not to scream, but finally it was too much. A groan formed into a scream, followed by another. Jonah stopped the current.

"Are you ready to tell her to cooperate? Beg her?" he asked.

"Never."

The pain started again. Reaching deep inside himself, Steve found something to hang onto—the memory of his transformation, the pain of the serum racing through his body, changing him cell by cell. He remembered how it had burned like fire in his veins, how he had felt it breaking him down before it built him back up again. Compared to that pain, this pain was like someone yelling in a distant room. Or so he told himself.

He must have blacked out again. When the world came back into focus, Jonah was frowning and shaking the Taser. The green lights were off, and all that was left was a blinking red LED.

Steve couldn't help himself, he laughed.

"You've run out of batteries?" he wheezed. "I'm sorry, but you have to admit, that's pretty funny."

He could hear Karl laughing too, and soon even Katherine joined in. Only Jonah didn't smile, and his eyes darted between the three of them. Anger twisted his face and he threw the Taser on the ground, hard. It shattered, and bits of plastic and metal flew everywhere.

"Laugh it up, but I have a dozen more just like that one. We'll see how funny it is when I get through using all of them on you." He stormed out of the room, leaving the three companions staring at each other.

"Well, Karl, I don't know about you, but I didn't enjoy that very much at all," Steve said.

Karl spat a mouthful of blood on the floor with an apologetic look.

"Where's your sense of adventure, Cap?" he asked. "At least it's never boring right?"

"How can you too be so . . . so . . . flippant?" Katherine demanded. "He'll be back soon, and what we will do then?"

"Katherine, we know that," Karl said gently. "Sometimes, all you can do is try not to think about what's coming next."

"There's nothing we can do right now," Steve said. "But, I've been in worse situations than this and come through the other side. We just have to endure and wait for an opportunity. It'll come; it always does."

"But you have to stay strong, Katherine," Karl said. "Steve and I can take this, but we need you to back us, okay?"

She nodded. "I hate this, but if that's what you want from me, then I'll try. Okay?"

"That's all we can ask," Steve said. While they had been talking, he had been pushing the wreckage of the Taser around with his foot. He grunted with satisfaction as he moved aside a couple of pieces of black plastic to reveal a stiff strand of copper wire. Gripping it between the toes of his boots, he shifted it around, trying to get it into a position to kick it up.

"An idea, Cap?" Karl asked. He had been watching Steve with interest. "A way out maybe?"

"Just a glimmer of hope, but it's better than nothing."

Karl nodded. But before Steve could give further thought to how he was going to get the piece of metal into his hands where he could give picking the restraints a go, the door slid open and Jonah came through it. He was pushing a stainless steel table on wheels, and on top of it were eight more Tasers.

"I lied, there weren't twelve. But, this should do the job."

He picked one up and pressed a button, smiling as the

green LEDs lit up, one by one. He was walking toward Steve when an alarm went off, filling the room with wailing sirens and strobing lights. A woman's voice echoed from the speakers in the ceiling.

"Security breach. I repeat security breach. All personnel to emergency stations. Code Red. This is not a drill."

As the captives stared at each other, the message repeated over and over.

Chapter 17

Jonah barked orders into his transceiver. The door slid open and the two guards rushed in. Jonah met them at the doorway.

"What's going on?" Steve heard him ask.

One of the guards said something in a low voice that even Steve couldn't catch, but a deaf man could have heard Jonah's reply.

"What?! How many?" He turned and looked the prisoners over. "We need to get the girl out of here. Grab her and bring her with me."

The guard murmured something else.

"Don't worry about the other two, they aren't going anywhere. We can come back for them once we've dealt with this little problem."

The two guards unfastened Katherine from her chair and dragged her over to Jonah.

"Wait, what are you doing?" She struggled against their grip, but they barely seemed to notice. "Steve! Karl!"

"It's okay, Katherine," Steve said. "We'll come after you as soon we can. I promise."

"Don't make promises you can't keep, Rogers," Jonah said. Pulling out a gag, he silenced Katherine's pleas, and bound her hands in front of her with efficient and clinical speed. He pushed her roughly into the guards' arms and followed them out the door, slamming it shut, and leaving Karl and Steve alone.

"Now what?" Karl asked.

"Well . . ." Steve rocked his chair back and forth. After a few oscillations, he crashed to the floor. He wriggled toward the wreckage of the Taser, then braced himself. With a convulsive heave, he flexed his abdominal muscles and used the incredible power of his core to flip himself and the chair over so that he could get at the copper wire with his hands. After a bit of fiddling, he had it in his grasp.

"Nice," Karl said admiringly.

It wasn't easy with the angle of his hands and the less than optimal lock pick he was using, but in less than five minutes, the restraints clicked open. Steve stood and stretched the kinks out of his muscles, and then got to work freeing Karl. With his own hands loose, it was a much quicker process. Karl staggered slightly when he stood, and Steve caught his arm to stop him from falling.

"Are you okay?" he asked.

"My legs feel a bit rubbery, and my body doesn't seem to

want to do what it's told, but other than that, I'm fine."

"Are you going to be able to keep up? I hate to be blunt, but we'll have to move fast."

"The day a Marine can't keep up with some Army boy . . . let's just say I would never be able to show my face at the VFW ever again."

"Let's get moving then," Steve said. "I don't know what's going on out there, but I want to get Katherine before anything else can go wrong."

As if to punctuate his words, there was an explosion followed by the sound of gunfire. Steve and Karl grabbed their shirts and jackets and quickly dressed, then looked around for anything that could be used as a weapon. The only options were the Tasers, and they grabbed a pair each and ran into the corridor. Karl labored slightly, but was as good as his word and kept up with Rogers.

They stopped off at the room that had been the site of Steve's initial interrogation so he could retrieve his shield, then continued on. As they rounded the corner, two guards almost ran straight into them. Without even needing to speak, Rogers broke right and Karl broke left. There was a crackle of electricity and the smell of ozone, and two bodies fell to the floor with a thump.

"It's more fun being on this end of it, isn't it?" Karl asked.

One of the security guards tried to get up on his elbows. Karl leaned down and grabbed him by the collar, pulling him up and forward. The guard's eyes went wide as electricity arced just under his nose.

"Where's the girl?" Karl yelled. "Tell me!"

The security guard hesitated for a moment.

"Don't test me! I've had the equivalent of the local power grid pumped through me and I'm not in the mood. Do you hear me?"

"Yes," the man stammered. "He's taken her to the bunker—it's three levels below here. There's a tunnel that leads out of here."

"And what's going on in here?" Steve demanded. "What are all the sirens about?"

"I don't know! Code Red means we have intruders—that's all I know, I swear!"

"Thank you, you've been very helpful," Karl said, then gave the guard another dose with the Taser. The man jerked once, then passed out.

"Was that necessary?" Steve asked.

"Yes," Karl said. "We can't have him following us. And I feel much better now."

"Fair enough," Steve said. "I would have been tempted myself. To the elevator?"

"After you."

As they ran toward the elevator, its doors slid open and a familiar figure stepped out, a white cloak rippling out behind him. When Taskmaster saw Steve stopping short, he paused and pulled the shield off his back.

"Karl, you need to get out of here," Steve said. "I'll take care of this, but you need to go after Katherine."

"Why don't we just take care of him together? It won't take long."

"Just go."

Even as the words were coming out of Steve's mouth, Taskmaster was on him. They traded blows faster than Karl's eyes could follow, shields flicking and clanging off one another, arms blocking vicious strikes. Karl's jaw dropped.

"Okay, I think I'll go take care of Katherine."

Steve threw his attacker over his shoulder, but Taskmaster simply hit the ground rolling, and came to his feet. Steve hadn't expected anything less, but had achieved what he'd wanted. The hallway was now clear for Karl to dart past them and get to the elevator. He hammered the button to close the door, raising a hand to wish Steve good luck as the doors closed.

"Now, it's just you and me, Taskmaster."

"Yes, and this time your little friend isn't here to save you," the man replied. "I've been looking forward to settling this score. The $2 million is just the icing on the cake."

"Who's going to pay you? I thought your paymasters already had her."

Taskmaster smiled. "There are lots of interested parties out there—word gets around in certain circles, you should know that. It's a seller's market. I might even end up getting more than the two million, but I'm more interested in wiping the floor with you. Call it professional pride. While my competitors are occupied with each other, I'm going to make the most of this opportunity."

He swept back his cloak, revealing the sword at his side. In a single fluid motion, he drew it and brought it whistling down in an overhand strike. Steve caught the sword on his shield, rolling his wrist so that the force of the blow was directed to the side, then stepped inside the man's reach and punched the inside of Taskmaster's elbow twice in quick succession, his middle knuckle sticking out. The sharp blows to the bundle of nerves had the desired effect, and Taskmaster's arm went numb, the sword dropping from his nerveless fingers. Steve kicked the weapon out of reach and threw another punch, this time going for Taskmaster's throat. But Taskmaster was too quick, and got a block up just in time, then brought his own knee crashing into the big muscle of Steve's thigh. Rogers staggered back, nearly tripping as his weight came down on the suddenly numb leg. Taskmaster was already at him, twirling into a series of roundhouse kicks, his heel whistling past Steve's chin again and again as Steve desperately retreated.

He felt the cold steel of the elevator doors at his back, and managed to catch the next kick, grabbing Taskmaster's foot and twisting so that the other man flipped over in midair. But Steve's attacker was like a cat, somehow managing to land in a crouch from which he launched himself back at Rogers. Steve took two punishing strikes to the ribs before he could get in one of his own—a vicious jab that split the skin above Taskmaster's left eye.

They broke apart and stood a moment, chests heaving as they regarded each other warily. Taskmaster brought his arms up and crossed them in front of his chest, rapping them together. With an audible click, a blade shot out from the back of each of his gauntlets, glimmering evilly in the fluorescent lighting.

Steve sighed. "Really? That's how you want to be?"

Rogers strapped his shield to his left arm, and pulled the two Tasers from his belt. Blue electricity crackled as he brought his hands up. With a wordless roar, Taskmaster attacked, blades flicking out so fast that they were mere blurs of metal. Steve caught some of the slashes on his shield, and deflected others with the reinforced arm braces embedded in the sleeves of his uniform. Inevitably, a few jabs made it through and Steve soon bled from half a dozen shallow cuts, but Taskmaster was unable to land a killing blow. Steve weathered the storm of steel, watching for a gap in his opponent's defenses, and when it came, he was ready. As Taskmaster lined up a backhand attack, Steve plunged his right hand through opening and pressed the Taser against Taskmaster's side, triggering the charge.

Taskmaster staggered and fell to one knee. Steve brought his own knee up, crashing it into his enemy's jaw and sending him tumbling back in a heap. Before Steve could press his advantage, the other man was up, but for the first time Steve saw uncertainty in his eyes, and there was a wariness in his next approach.

Taskmaster stumbled slightly as he closed again with Steve. Rogers took advantage of the momentary lapse to drop into a vicious leg sweep, knocking Taskmaster's legs out from underneath him and landing him flat on his back. Instead of lying prone, though, Taskmaster flexed his back, giving himself enough momentum to get his feet underneath him. As he straightened his torso back to vertical, Steve's fist met Taskmaster's chin and sent him straight back down.

But it still wasn't enough to stop the man. Using the wall to bring himself to his feet, Taskmaster met Steve's renewed attack. And now he had begun to memorize the patterns of Steve's technique, leaving Rogers feeling like he was fighting a mirror image of himself. Every time he threw a punch or a kick, Taskmaster seemed to be waiting for it. Nothing Steve threw at him seemed to surprise him. Again, Steve tried all of the tricks and techniques he had picked up from those he had fought alongside or against, but Taskmaster was the equal of them all.

As the fight continued, Steve could feel the events of the past week catching up with him. He hadn't fully recovered from his last beating at the hands of this foe, and the torture had only exacerbated things. Now, with each blow, it took him just a little longer to bounce back, and his reaction times were just that little bit slower. It was only a matter of time before the balance of conflict would tip catastrophically in Taskmaster's favor—unless Steve could come up with something soon.

As he continued to defend himself, Steve racked his brain, trying to remember everything he knew about Taskmaster. He knew from their last encounter that Taskmaster had memorized the techniques of a wide range of fighters, many of whom Steve assumed the villain had actually fought. But he'd also already seemed familiar with Steve's style even before they'd started fighting, so Steve had to think that Taskmaster had studied footage of Captain America; there was certainly enough of it on the news or floating around the internet. He thought quickly, knowing his only chance was to find a technique that Taskmaster couldn't have seen.

While he warded off Taskmaster's counterattack, a memory came back to Steve from the days before he had been Captain America, when he had simply been Steve Rogers. Instead of being faster and stronger than those around him, he had been a weakling, prey to the neighborhood bullies. Not a week had gone by that he hadn't come home with a bloodied nose or a split lip, until one day his best friend had decided he'd seen enough. Bucky had been everything Steve was not—muscular, athletic, and popular with the girls. He'd defended Steve when he could, but he'd also taught Steve some dirty tricks for when he couldn't, and to rely on his brains instead of trying to match his opponent's brawn. Right now, Rogers was a long way from the tough streets of New York where they'd grown up, and Steve could only hope Taskmaster had never been in a street fight on the Lower East Side.

Steve began to favor his right arm, wincing every time he threw a punch and deliberately pulling back the power of his blows, and reacting just the slightest bit slower when he used that arm to block, giving the occasional gasp of pain on impact. Taskmaster noticed the apparent weakness, and focused his attacks on Steve's right side, pressing home his advantage. Steve fell back step after step, allowing Taskmaster to drive him toward the wall. Growing in confidence, Taskmaster ignored his defense, throwing punch after punch at Rogers, raining down blow after blow on Steve's right side. Finally, he overextended one time too many, and Steve's left hand darted out, grabbing the other man's shirt.

Caught off balance, Taskmaster could do nothing as Steve pulled him in close and slammed his forehead into the bridge of Taskmaster's nose with all the power he could summon. With a sickening crunch, the cartilage broke and blood gushed from the man's nose. Taskmaster staggered back, dropping his guard, and Steve took his chance, slamming his first brutally into the other man's stomach. Winded, Taskmaster battled to block the barrage of punches as Steve worked him over, fists pounding into the other man's ribs and torso again and again. Finally, Taskmaster slumped forward and Steve caught him, pulling him into another head butt, even more vicious than the last. This time, Taskmaster's eyes rolled up into his head and he went limp in Steve's grip. Rogers let him fall, and staggered back to lean against the wall, gasping for breath.

"That's what we called a 'Bucky kiss,' back in the good old days. One of the many important lessons he taught me."

The only reply he got was Taskmaster's labored breathing, and Steve sighed in relief. He hadn't wanted to kill the man, only put him out of commission.

"I'm sorry I can't hang around to chat, but I really do have someplace else to be. What am I going to do with you, though?"

Steve ran back down the corridor to where he and Karl had left the guards. Rolling one of them over, Steve grabbed the handcuffs hanging on his belt. Taskmaster scrabbled weakly at Steve's hands as Rogers pulled the man's hands behind his back, but he was too weak to resist, and Steve soon had him securely bound. He dragged Taskmaster into one of the cells and fastened him to a chair.

"That should keep you out of trouble."

Rogers ran into the elevator and peered at the control panel. There was no mystery—the bottom button was labeled *Bunker*. Steve could only wish that all of the villains he had fought over the years had been so considerate. But, labeling it a bunker did little to prepare Steve for the sheer size of it when the elevator doors opened. The space had once been a vast, natural cavern almost the size and shape of a football field, and it was still dotted with stalactites and stalagmites the size of redwoods. But the natural features of the cavern were obscured by platforms that had been built around them or suspended from the cavern roof. This created several levels of storage, where Steve could make out weapons racks and shelves of food.

The closest platform to the elevator was attached to the roof by thick metal pylons, so that at first sight it seemed to float unsupported, almost directly above Steve. His view was limited by the angle, but he could make out what looked like a smaller version of the control room upstairs. The only way up was a set of steel stairs that were currently retracted and stowed on the platform itself, almost twenty-five feet off the ground.

Steve didn't have much time to take in the engineering feats of the cavern. There were soldiers everywhere, some in the anonymous black of Ex Umbra, but they were coming under heavy fire from a new group, and these soldiers bore the familiar S.H.I.E.L.D. insignia. The Ex Umbra troops were holding the platforms farther in the cavern, laying down blankets of withering fire as S.H.I.E.L.D. forces tried to advance using every available feature of the cavern as cover. Behind him, he could hear S.H.I.E.L.D. reinforcements pouring from the stairwells on either side of the elevator.

Steve scanned the rest of the cavern in the hope of finding his companions. At its far end was a pair of massive steel doors built into the rock of the cave wall, on either side of which a mix of vehicles ranging from jeeps and motorcycles to a number of the ubiquitous M35 cargo trucks—the model commonly known as a deuce and a half—were lined up. All of the vehicles were neatly arranged and the spaces were all full, giving no sign of a hasty exodus, and leading Steve to hope he was not too late.

The opposing forces' attention was on the occupied platforms, and Steve was able to make his way unobserved to the stalagmite on the other side of the control platform. Movement above him caught his eye, and he looked up to see Karl and Jonah facing off. Jonah sported a large purple bruise on the side of his face and blood trickled from his nose. He pointed a pistol up into the beams of the artificial ceiling that arched over the platform, and where Steve could just make out the shadowy form of Katherine wedged into the angle where two beams met. Her arms were bound in front of her and she was gagged, and Steve realized Karl must have lifted her up there in an attempt to keep her safe. Steve pulled his shield from his back and sent it skimming through the air. He'd aimed for Jonah's head, but at the last minute Jonah turned, perhaps distracted by the flicker of motion at the corner of his eye. The shield hit his gun instead, knocking it neatly out of his hand and sending it spinning off the edge of the platform, while the shield ricocheted and returned to Steve's hand.

From where he stood, Steve could hear Jonah's curse, and Rogers watched as the former S.H.I.E.L.D. agent pulled out the twin staves he had wielded so well during their earlier encounter. The Tasers in Karl's hands looked insubstantial in comparison, and Steve looked around for a way to get up to help him, a remote control for the stairs, anything. As he watched, Jonah launched a blistering attack, staves flickering out. Karl danced back, weaving out of the way of each strike, but Steve could see it was only a matter of time before one connected. He pulled his shield from his back, but was unable to get a clear throw at Jonah as the two combatants wheeled around each other.

One of the staves came down on Karl's forearm with a sickening snap loud enough to carry all the way to the ground. Steve winced as he watched Karl trying not to let what must have been excruciating pain slow him down. Jonah drove him back toward the edge of the platform, each lunge sending Karl back another step; he was slowly but surely running out of room. Steve's eyes flicked up to the roof above the two men, his attention caught by Katherine's stealthy movements. Inch by inch, she crept along the beam, hampered by her bonds. Twice she slipped and almost fell, and Steve could only imagine the determination that was keeping her going. Moving along the beam would have been hard enough on its own, but with her hands tied, she had no way of steadying herself—or of protecting herself should she fall.

Finally, she was directly above the combatants, and she slowly straightened, her body quivering with the effort. She stood motionless for a moment, and Steve's perfect vision could make out how wide her eyes were. She took a deep breath, then, just as Jonah wound back his arm to deliver the coup de grâce, dropped from the roof. Her feet hit Jonah square between the shoulders, driving him face first into the steel floor before she tumbled off to the side. Jonah started to lift himself up, and then collapsed, lying motionless. Katherine staggered to her feet, and stumbled over to Karl, who simply stood, cradling his arm and staring at her in amazement. She fell against him, and he wrapped his good arm around her in a clumsy embrace.

Chapter 18

Steve waited for the stairs to descend, and the moment they touched the ground he almost ran up them.

"Katherine, Karl, are you okay?"

"Thanks to her we are," Karl said, looking at Katherine with naked admiration. "I thought I was in a bit of trouble there. Talk about b—, I mean, guts."

Steve had already freed Katherine's mouth from the gag, and she gave Karl a weak smile before gasping at the pain of blood flow returning to her hands as Steve removed her restraints. He turned to Karl, who winced as Steve checked his forearm, gently running his hand along the ex-Marine's forearm. It was a clean break, and Steve quickly bound it with a strip of cloth ripped from Jonah's shirt, and fashioned a sling using the unconscious man's belt. Jonah was out cold and showed no signs of stirring.

"I don't think we need to worry about him waking up anytime soon," Steve said. "You really did a number on him."

"Think that's good, you should have seen her before,"

Karl said. "When I caught up with them, he had a gun on her. She managed to twist free and club him in the face with her bound hands. She got up one of those pylons before he could recover."

"Couldn't let you two have all the fun," Katherine said. "So, where to now?"

"Out those big doors?" Karl asked.

Steve shook his head. "I have no idea how to open them, or where they even go. Plus, I want to cause some mayhem on the way out. I vote we head back up and see what mischief we can get up to."

"Speaking of mayhem, I see you managed to deal with your friend," Karl said. He leaned over and pulled the gun from Jonah's shoulder holster.

"Your friend?" Katherine asked in confusion. "What are you talking about?"

"Remember the guy who gate-crashed our apartment?" She nodded. "He came back looking for a rematch."

"How did you manage without me to help you out?"

"With great difficulty," Steve said, smiling. "Don't get too cocky, though, just because you laid out Jonah here."

"I'll do my best," she said.

Suddenly a huge explosion blew out the big doors at the far end of the cavern, sending vehicles flying. One of the cargo trucks flipped end over end, coming to rest in pyre of black smoke and fire. More S.H.I.E.L.D. troops poured in through the rent, laying down withering fire on the Ex Umbra troops. Reinforced, the S.H.I.E.L.D. forces started clearing the platforms one by one, but the defenders fought with undiminished ferocity, only giving ground slowly. Even as the platforms were cleared, the Ex Umbra forces used the boulders and stalagmites that littered the cavern floor as cover, fighting with the skill of troops on familiar terrain. As the currents of the battle swept toward Steve and his friends, bullets pinged off the railings of the control platform, and the companions threw themselves to the steel floor.

For a moment, Steve entertained thoughts of trying to simply sneak past the troops to make their escape, but seeing the soldiers in the S.H.I.E.L.D. insignia under fire reminded him of too many past battles at their side. He couldn't abandon them; it just wasn't in him to do so. Rogers turned back to the other two and held a finger to his lips, and then gestured for them to follow him. They crept around the perimeter, keeping out of a direct line of sight, until they were directly behind the biggest pocket of Ex Umbra holdouts. The Ex Umbra forces had found cover among a group of boulders, and from this impregnable position were able to prevent the S.H.I.E.L.D. forces from advancing farther.

Steve turned to Karl. "Lay down some covering fire."

"What are you going to do?"

Steve ignored his question. "Ready? Now!"

Using his good hand, Karl fired off a few shots, kicking

up puffs of smoke and splinters of rock to either side of the enemy. Even before Karl had pulled the trigger, Steve had leaped from the platform, ducking into a commando roll. Using his momentum, he kept moving, sprinting from boulder to boulder, then launching himself into the midst of the Ex Umbra fighters. He carved through them in a whirlwind of red, white, and blue, fists crunching into body armor and his shield deflecting attack after attack. Mere minutes later, he stood alone, surrounded by the bodies of his fallen enemies, his shield raised and shoulders squared.

"Who's next?" he asked, looking around the bunker.

Seeing their last hope conquered, the last few pockets of Ex Umbra surrendered, and soon the area was silent save for the clink of metal as the defeated forces stacked their weapons under the hard, watchful eyes of the S.H.I.E.L.D. operatives.

Cautiously, Katherine and Karl moved to join Steve. Weapons tracked their progress until one of the S.H.I.E.L.D. operatives stepped forward and gestured for everyone to lower their guns. Whoever it was, they were clad in bulky body armor and a state-of-the-art combat helmet covered their face with a bulletproof plexiglass visor. It was only when they removed the helmet that Steve realized it was Maria. She looked at him levelly, and nodded.

"Captain."

"Maria."

Then Katherine ran past him.

"Aunt Maria!"

She threw her arms around Maria, who awkwardly returned her embrace, patting her on the back.

"Hello, Katherine, it's good to see you," she said. "I'm glad you're okay."

Katherine stepped back and smiled at her.

"Only just. It's been a wild ride."

Maria looked at Karl. "And this is?"

"This is Karl," Steve said. "We wouldn't have gotten this far without him."

"Not sure that's true, but I'll take the credit," Karl said.

"Karl? Do you have a last name?" Maria asked.

"Karl is just fine for now, ma'am," he replied, eyes suddenly flat and watchful.

"That's fine," Maria said.

There was an awkward silence, and Steve stepped forward.

"Maria, you're a sight for sore eyes. But, I'm curious—how did you find us? And how are you going to be able to justify a raid on a government facility?"

Steve could have sworn Maria flushed slightly.

"Are you sure you want me to answer that, Steve?" she asked. "We might be better off leaving it alone."

"What do you mean?" Steve asked, baffled. "Why would that be better?"

"Because you aren't going to be happy with the answer. Not happy at all."

"Try me."

She stepped closer to him and reached under his uniform's cuff, pulling out a black sphere no more than three or four times the size of the head of a match.

"What is that?" Steve asked. "Is that a tracking device? Have you been tracking me?"

Maria wouldn't meet his eye.

"That's not just a tracking device," Karl said. "That's a very expensive piece of technology that doesn't simply transmit a tracking signal, but that also acts as a very sensitive microphone."

Steve's head jerked around.

"What are you saying, Karl?"

"That they haven't just been tracking you, Cap, they've been listening in on you."

"Is this true, Maria? Did you bug me?" Steve could feel himself starting to get angry, and he deliberately tried to tamp it down—but it was still there, waiting.

"Steve, you have to understand . . ."

"Is it true?" Now the anger was in his voice, flat and dangerous. "Have you been bugging me?"

"Yes, Steve, we have," Maria said. "I'm sorry. I planted that on the sleeve of your jacket at the warehouse. I knew that you have it with you almost all the time."

"I don't understand," Steve said. "Why would you do something like that without telling me?"

"Well, it worked out for the best, didn't it?" she asked defensively. "It meant we knew where you were and we could come in guns blazing. And, most importantly, we got recordings of Jonah admitting to extralegal behavior far beyond the bounds of anything he had been authorized to carry out, and even committing violations of a number of treaties by torturing prisoners. It gave me the proof I needed to go all the way to the top and get the authorization to shut this operation down. Ex Umbra is finished. They've embarrassed too many other agencies, and gone far beyond what any politician will turn a blind eye to, and that means whatever political capital they had has evaporated."

"That's not the point!" Steve was almost yelling. "You had no right to do that without my knowledge. I don't work for you."

"No, Captain, you don't." Her tone was clipped and precise. "But you work for the United States government. You should remember that."

"I'm not your stooge."

"I made a decision based on the situation. I'm sorry that you're unhappy with it, but I stand by it. Without that proof, the agents Ex Umbra have in place would have been able to stop any investigation before it started, or could have made me disappear. But once I got the recording into the right hands, all this became too big to cover up—even for them."

Steve and Maria glared at each other. Katherine stepped between them, raising her hands in a calming gesture.

"Let's all calm down, okay? Aunt Maria, that was definitely not cool, you know that? Steve, she was just trying to keep us safe."

"I'm still not very happy about it, but I guess I can't do much about it now," Steve said. "But don't you ever do anything like that to me again. Do you understand?"

Maria nodded, but before she could say anything else, he cut her off.

"You've spent all this time teaching yourself not to trust anyone, Maria," Steve said. "But, no one can do everything on their own, not even you. Sometimes you have to take a chance and rely on someone else—I've learned that the hard way. If you'd just asked me to wear a bug, don't you think I would have said yes? How can I trust *you* now?"

Maria opened her mouth to reply, but was interrupted by the sight of Jonah being dragged over to her. He stumbled, supported by the S.H.I.E.L.D. guards on either side of him, but there was no fear in his eyes as he met Maria's gaze.

"What's the meaning of this, Hill? How dare you?" he spat. "I'll have your head for this. In fact, I'll have S.H.I.E.L.D. shut down."

"I think not," Maria said coldly. "It's Ex Umbra that is finished."

Jonah went pale. "How do you know that name?"

She nodded at Steve. "You can thank the captain for that."
Steve didn't reply, and simply glared at her.

"We've suspected the existence of Ex Umbra for years now, but I'll give you credit, you lived up to your name. However, if you'd been content to stay in the shadows, we might never have crossed paths." Maria continued, ignoring Steve's look, "But you crossed a line when you suborned some of my operatives and used them against us. We'd cleaned house, gotten rid of people who were corruptible, but we didn't count on another agency of our own government appealing to people's patriotism. Jonah, you were one of us. How could you use your history with S.H.I.E.L.D. against us?"

"I was serving my country the best I could," Jonah said. "S.H.I.E.L.D. doesn't go far enough."

"And Ex Umbra goes too far," Maria said. "It's over. We have more than enough evidence of you going beyond the law. I have a recording of you engaging in the torture of US citizens and admitting to attempted murder. Your problem is, you talk too much."

She pulled out a piece of paper embossed with an extravagant seal. Unfolding it, she held it in front of Jonah's face, and he blanched.

"I take it you recognize the signature?" she asked, and he nodded. "There is no higher authority you can appeal to than the president. You and your men are under arrest." She gestured to two of her agents. "Take him away."

As Jonah was marched off, she turned to Steve.

"See, that's why I did what I did," she said. "And as a result, Ex Umbra are finished. Don't you see that it was worth it?"

"Careful, Maria," Steve said coldly. "Thinking that the end justifies the means is what made Ex Umbra what they were."

She flushed. "It's not the same."

"You can tell yourself that, Maria," he said. "But, I think we should be leaving. We've got some decisions to make. Maria, I'll be in touch. Now that you have Jonah, you'll be able to make sure there are no remnants of Ex Umbra left anywhere, and when you've confirmed S.H.I.E.L.D. is no longer compromised, we can talk about what happens next."

"I'm afraid I can't let you do that," Maria said softly.

"What?" Steve asked.

Katherine and Karl stared at her.

"I can't let you leave," she repeated.

"Aunt Maria, is this some sort of joke?" Katherine asked. "If it is, it isn't funny."

"It's no joke," Karl said. "We should have seen this coming."

"Maria, I don't know what this is about, but we are leaving," Steve said carefully. "It's not up for debate."

"I'm sorry, Steve, I can't let you do that."

"And how are you planning on stopping me?"

Maria gave a small sigh of resignation and signaled her

troops with a slight hand gesture. Suddenly, a dozen guns were trained on Steve and his companions.

"That's how."

"You wouldn't seriously shoot us," Katherine said. "You're bluffing. You must be."

"We'd only shoot if we had no other choice," Maria replied. "Most of those guns are carrying nonlethal rounds."

"Most?" Karl asked.

"I have orders that on no account am I allowed to let you go," Maria said. "I would much rather you just come along with us peacefully, or in the worst case, incapacitated. But, the orders were clear, I am to take any measures necessary."

Katherine looked like a kid who had just been told that Santa wasn't real, an expression of complete and utter disillusionment on her face.

"How could you do this, Aunt Maria? You promised you would protect me."

"And I have. I provided you with the best bodyguard on the planet, someone who would never even dream of abandoning you, or selling you out, or breaking his word that he would keep you safe. Even with the evidence from the bug getting this raid sanctioned, I still had to call in more favors than you can imagine to make it happen so fast. And now I'm going to take you someplace safe."

"You mean you're going to force me to go with you."

"If I have to." There was no hint of uncertainty in Maria's

voice whatsoever, no wavering, just an air of implacability.

"Don't do this, Maria," Steve said. "How can you guarantee Jonah doesn't have any sleepers planted just waiting for something like this? You don't know what he's capable of the way I do. He's a fanatic who has surrounded himself with zealots, and they aren't simply going to turn themselves in. You can't keep her safe out there. I can."

"I don't have a choice. You of all people should understand that, Steve. I took an oath, and I take it very seriously. I have to put my obligations and responsibilities above my own personal desires, above friendships, above family," Maria said. "I simply can't see any other choice here. Unless they violate certain moral or ethical standards, I can't just pick and choose what orders I obey—and I don't think this one violates anything."

"What?" Karl said. "You've got to be kidding me."

"What would you know?" Maria demanded, rounding on him. For the first time, Steve could see how much strain this was putting on her, and how tightly she was keeping her emotions on a leash. "Are you across all the contracts Katherine signed when she started working for S.H.I.E.L.D.? She agreed that her research belonged to us. She signed NDAs. You know what? S.H.I.E.L.D. could quite legally make the case she's stolen from the organization, and charge her under a number of Acts."

Karl didn't have anything to say in return.

"You have to understand, all of you, that this is not what I want, but I don't see any other choice."

"You don't see any moral imperative here, Maria?" Steve asked. "You don't think it's important enough to justify disobeying orders—that this goes beyond governments?"

"I don't think I'm qualified to decide that, Steve," she said. "I don't think any of us are."

"Then who is?" Karl asked.

"I don't know," Maria replied. "All I know is that I'm going to obey my orders. If I were to do otherwise, I wouldn't be fit for command. In fact, I would deserve to have my command taken away from me and given to someone else who would do their job properly."

She looked directly at Steve.

"Do you understand what I'm saying?"

"I think I do," Steve said slowly. "You've made it very clear."

He turned to the other two.

"Look, Maria is just doing her job; how about we make easy on her and go along with them?"

"What?!" Karl and Katherine said at the same time, sounding like a cut-rate Greek chorus.

"Cap, you can't be serious," Karl said, sounding shocked at Steve's change of heart. "We can find another way out of this. Just say the word."

"I am serious. I think our best bet is to go with them—let S.H.I.E.L.D. sort this out."

"I can't believe this. I thought we had talked through this, come to an understanding about this. It's not even about me—you know that this is bigger than S.H.I.E.L.D., that they don't have the right to decide what happens to it. It belongs to the world!" Katherine said. She sounded like she was trying not to cry. "How could you do this to me? Either of you?"

Steve took Katherine's hand. She tried to pull away, but he wouldn't let her.

"Katherine, I know you don't understand, but I'm asking you to trust me one more time. Please."

He squeezed her hand, and then let her go.

"Will you do that, please?"

She nodded grudgingly.

"Okay, Steve—one last time."

Karl looked he was going to say something, but at a look from Steve, he subsided. Steve turned back to Maria.

"Okay, I guess we're going with you."

"Thank you, Steve. Katherine, I hope you'll realize it was the only option."

A pair of S.H.I.E.L.D. operatives bracketed each of the companions and led them after Maria as she headed toward the stairway. When they tried the elevator, it had stopped working. The control panel wouldn't even light up, and the S.H.I.E.L.D. operatives covering them gestured for them to take the stairs. Katherine was the only one who seemed unfazed by the flights stretching out in front of them. Both men had taken too many beatings in too short a time to enjoy the physical exertion. As they climbed, they could see through the glass windows on the doors of each landing, and they took in the evidence of heavy fighting. The hallways were deserted, but more often than not there were unconscious—or dead—bodies littering the floor. After what seemed like hours, they came to the final floor.

"This is it," Maria said.

"It had to be the last one, didn't it?" Karl puffed. "If I find out who killed the elevators, I'm going to shoot him in the kneecaps."

"Karl!" Katherine said, sounding shocked. "That's awful!"

"I'm kidding!" he said, then muttered, "Mostly."

The bustling control room that Steve had been escorted past only a few hours before was gone, and what was left was unrecognizable. There was a gaping hole in the roof with a number of drop lines hanging down, and all around the room tables and chairs were scattered as if a tornado had swept through. Maria gave the order, and soon the three companions had been fitted with harnesses and clipped to the lines hanging from the roof. She spoke into a transceiver, and the lines rose, taking the companions with them, and in a matter of minutes, they stood on the roof of the building. They were in the middle of a forested canyon, the building built into the slope of the mountain.

The roof had its own helipad, and a S.H.I.E.L.D. helicopter rested there, waiting. The helicopter was at the cutting edge of technology, all stealth material and graceful curves. It looked like nothing more than a huge wasp, all the way down to its tapered tail.

At a gesture from Maria, the three companions were bundled on board and strapped into their seats. Only after they were safely restrained did Maria slide in and sit across from them.

"Don't worry, you won't be stuck there for long. It's only a thirty-minute flight in one of these things. I hope none of you get airsick—we're going to be flying low and fast, and that means that we'll be dodging everything from tall buildings to large trees. It's like threading the needle at about three hundred miles an hour."

No one said anything, and Maria sighed.

"Okay, I get that you're mad at me. How about I leave you all to it?"

She clambered over the seats and into the front of the cockpit, sitting next to the pilot. She put on her headset, and then flashed him a thumbs-up. The pilot flicked some switches, and the engines revved with a low whine. It was surprisingly quiet, nothing like the choppers Steve was used to. It was nice being able to hear himself think.

"So, are you sure about this, Cap?" Karl asked. "You've got a plan, right?"

"Not really," Steve replied, "But we don't really have a choice. It's a bit late now, anyway."

He was right—the chopper was already lifting off, so smoothly that it felt more like being in a hot air balloon than in a helicopter. As the Ex Umbra base fell away behind them, Steve could not help but wonder whether they had merely exchanged one kind of danger for another. He looked at Karl and Katherine. They had been through so much together, and even now, despite this setback, he could feel the faith they had in him. He watched the scenery outside whip by, the chopper traveling too fast for him to make out any details of what they were passing. As they hurtled toward S.H.I.E.L.D. headquarters, he promised himself that he would be worthy of their faith, and that he would do whatever he could to ensure that they all came out the other side of this—together.

Chapter 19

Another day, another interrogation room; this was becoming just a normal part of Steve's routine. *At least this one has more comfortable chairs*, Steve thought as he regarded the woman sitting across from him. She met his gaze without flinching.

"So, should I call my lawyer, Maria?" Steve asked. "When do I get my phone call?"

"Oh, you aren't under arrest, Steve. Nothing so serious. You're just being detained."

"Detained?"

"That's right. We have all sorts of wide-ranging powers now, you know. In cases affecting national security, we can detain people without arresting them."

"And how does detaining someone differ from arresting them? Can they just leave whenever they want?"

"Of course not."

"Then . . . ?"

Maria smiled, but there was no humor in it whatsoever.

"We don't have to worry about things like phone calls or lawyers," she paused, "Or trials."

"What a brave new world," Steve muttered. "And how long can you hold them for? Hold me for?"

"As long as we want, really."

"And you think that this is okay? That that's how it should work?"

"Steve, what I think has nothing to do with it," Maria said. "I might find the whole thing repugnant, but I can't change it."

"If everyone thought like that, nothing would ever change, Maria."

"I've always admired your principles, Steve."

She was dodging the conversation, and Steve could see it, but he decided to let it slide for now.

"So, what happens now?" he asked instead. "How long will you 'detain' us for?"

"You? About another hour. The paperwork is being processed as we speak, and as soon as it arrives, you'll be free to go."

Steve narrowed his eyes.

"That seemed very specific. What about Katherine and Karl? Are they being released with me?"

"Karl is a member of an organization listed as a terrorist threat. He isn't going anywhere for a while."

"He's also a decorated Marine, without whom you never would have put an end to Ex Umbra. He was just as big a part of this as I was."

"And that will be taken into account. I'm sure that once it's all sorted out, he'll be free to go, too."

"And what about Katherine?" Steve asked. "I notice you've avoided mentioning her."

Maria flushed. "You know the answer to that. She isn't going anywhere, especially not until we understand how her discovery works so we can re-create her work for ourselves. It's too important just to let it walk out the door."

"It? What's this 'it' business?" Steve asked, his voice harsh with anger. "You mean *her*, Maria, you won't let *her* walk out the door. So much for how much she matters to you."

"Steve, I—"

"Maria, we go back a long way, so I'm going give you one warning. I'm not leaving Katherine, or Karl, behind," Steve said. "That's not how it works. One way or another, I won't be walking out of here alone."

"Steve, what exactly do you think I should do, then?" At the expression on his face, she hurriedly continued. "No, no, that's not a rhetorical question, or me trying to be smart. I honestly want to know. I don't know what I should do. Or what I can do."

"Aren't you the boss?" Steve asked. "Don't you get to decide?"

"One of the sad truths of life is that sometimes the more authority you have, the less freedom you have make your own decisions. I have so many guidelines I have to follow, and there are people I report to—yeah, I'm a boss, but I have one of my own, too." Maria suddenly looked very tired. "You know how this works better than anyone, Steve—I don't just give orders, I have to take them, too. Like the order to arrest you. If I'd refused, someone else would have done it. That was made very clear to me."

Steve nodded—he'd been right, Maria had been warning him in the bunker that it was either surrender to her, or surrender to someone else.

"So, what if you got to choose, though? No orders from anyone else, just your own call. What would you do?"

"I don't know, Steve, I really don't. The more I learn about this research, the more powerful it seems to me. It's a dangerous thing to have out there—maybe it's better to have it in our hands." She sighed. "Like I said, I admire your principles . . . and Katherine's. Part of me agrees with them. But, I have to weigh what this research means to national security, and I can't take that lightly."

"Lucky you don't have to bear the burden of making that decision then," Steve said.

"I can see in your eyes that you're disappointed with me, Steve."

"No, I just think you're wrong. I had this discussion with

Jonah, though this conversation has been a bit more pleasant than that one was. Some things are bigger than national security. In fact, they're bigger than any one nation. When Katherine first started telling me about this, I thought along the lines of what it would mean for the United States. But then I started, I mean, *really* started, to think about it."

"And what conclusion did you arrive at?"

"I thought about what this country stands for, what I love about it. To me, at its very heart, the idea of America is freedom. When people first started coming here, they wanted a place where they could be free. That's why people kept pushing west as things got more regulated—so they could continue to be free. Sometimes, I think we've lost sight of that idea."

He stopped, aware that Maria was watching him strangely. "What?"

"Nothing, keep going. Please."

"And to me, that's one of the things the war was about. I mean my war, World War Two." Steve paused, shaking his head. "I still sometimes forget that I can't just say 'the war' and expect people to know what I mean—but for me, that will always be the one. The one that changed my life. Changed everything, really."

"Don't worry, I knew what you meant."

"Anyway, in my mind, that's what we had more of than anyone—freedom. And there was a war going on, and all these countries at risk of losing what freedom they had to people bent on taking it away from them. And I thought to myself, if you have more of something that other people need, isn't sharing it the right thing to do? I wasn't much more than a kid, and it seemed to me that we had more freedom than anyone, and we needed to give it to the world."

He shook his head ruefully.

"I'm probably not making much sense."

"Don't worry, Steve, you're making plenty of sense."

"I've given everything for this country because I believe in what we stand for. As sappy as it may sound, I believe that when we're at our best, we're a beacon of hope and freedom in the world. And what's this thing that Katherine has created if not freedom itself? So many people around the world don't have the freedom that we take for granted, but this tool would go a long way to changing that."

He leaned forward, his eyes burning with his belief in what he was saying.

"What's the point of this American dream of ours if we don't want to share it with the rest of the world? When I realized that, that's when I realized that keeping this a secret would be betraying that dream."

"Wow, Steve, that was quite a speech." Maria seemed genuinely moved, her face slightly flushed. "Makes me wish it were up to me, that I could release this into the world."

"So do I, Maria." He gave her a penetrating look. "In

fact, I think that if you could have done anything about it, you already have would have, but I think you were worried that if you gave the order to let us go, it would have been disobeyed—that you might even have been relieved of command."

"I can't comment on that," Maria said. "But one thing I can tell you, is that this has been preying on my mind a lot, Steve. Please believe that. In fact, I've been so distracted that I've started making silly mistakes."

"What sort of mistakes?"

"Like coming into an interrogation room alone with one of the most dangerous men on the planet, who I had to arrest because of his very public attempt to defy my orders, and who has since told me that he isn't going to leave without his friends, and I didn't even make sure he was in restraints? Or, what about only posting three guards in the corridor—the same corridor that has two other interrogation rooms that are both occupied right now. Pretty careless stuff."

Steve watched her very carefully, weighing her words.

"Yes, that is extremely careless," he said. "Who knows what could happen as a result of poor decisions like that."

"Exactly. I mean someone could leap over the table and take my gun, knock me out with it—hell, they could even take my pass—you know, the one that opens every door in this building."

"Heaven forbid."

"It's embarrassing. The only reason I'm comfortable telling you about this is that we've known each other so long. Plus, the audio in this particular room isn't working. There's a video feed, but that's all."

"So, people can make sure there haven't been any incidents, but can't make out your conversation. Inconvenient."

"Very. Of course, if such an escape like that were to happen, I would hope the escapee would make it as quick and painless as something like that could be."

"Of course."

Steve nodded to her and tried to look apologetic before he launched himself over the desk at her. He didn't know whether it was professional pride, or if she was trying to make it convincing for the camera, but she got in a few good blows before he managed to wrestle her gun away from her. She landed one more punch before he rapped her on the temple with the butt of the pistol and she collapsed across the table. He looked down at her, wiping blood off his upper lip.

"Sorry about that."

He threw the gun into the corner and grabbed Maria's pass. A glimmer of red and blue in the corner of his eye caught his attention, and he walked over to where his shield was propped up against the wall.

"How considerate!"

Steve collected his shield and opened the door. As he did so, alarms rang, a steady, deep klaxon note—obviously someone had been paying attention to the video feed. He ran down the corridor, slamming into the first of the guards as he tried to pull out his gun. Steve punched him in the jaw, and the guard fell to floor. The next man was far enough away that he got his gun out, so Steve simply sent his shield flying down the corridor, bouncing from wall to wall until it smacked into the guard.

Steve scanned the hallway, wondering where the third guard was. He got his answer a moment later when the man came out of one of the doors with an arm around Karl's neck and a gun jammed into his temple.

"I'm sorry, Cap, but you have to put your hands up." The guard's voice was shaking. "I don't want to hurt anyone, especially not you, but I can't just let you go."

Steve raised his hands, but before he could place them on his head, the guard toppled to the ground. Katherine stood over him, clutching a snapped-off chair arm.

"That's both of you I've saved so far," she crowed. "Idiots. They thought I didn't need a guard. When I heard the commotion out here, I smashed up the chair and came running."

"Good work," Steve said. "But we don't have much time to bask in your reflected glory. We have to get out of here."

"How are we going to do that, Cap?" Karl asked. "This place must be locked down tight."

Steve held up Maria's pass.

"Let's just say I had some help from a friend."

Despite the alarms, it was surprisingly easy going. Maria's pass that meant that they could enter any area of the building. Any time that they heard approaching footsteps, they would simply duck through another door. When they did encounter guards, they were generally so surprised to see them in restricted areas that Karl and Steve were able to deal with them quietly. Still, Steve breathed a sigh of relief when they made it to the elevator and rode it down to the car park. They'd managed to make it out without hurting anyone— which pleased Steve, as harming S.H.I.E.L.D. operatives simply doing what they thought was their job was something he would have found hard to live with.

It only took moments for Karl to jimmy his way into one of the vehicles and hot-wire it to life.

"Where'd you learn to do that?" Katherine asked.

"Here and there." Karl grinned. "Best thing about it is that it means that I get to drive."

"Shotgun!" Katherine said.

Once she explained to Steve what that meant, they got going, rubber squealing as Karl floored the accelerator. Ahead, the roller door slowly descended.

"This is going to be close," Karl yelled. "Buckle up and say your prayers."

His hands were white on the wheel, and Steve and Katherine hurriedly fastened their seat belts and ducked down low. The rectangle of light grew narrower, and then they were under it with a terrible screeching as the roof of the car was scraped clean of paint, enamel, and a layer of metal. But they were through, hurtling down the street, with Karl handling the car like a pro.

They drove a few blocks before switching cars—Karl pulling up beside another motorist at a light and Steve hopping out, apologizing to the stunned occupant and explaining that they needed the car for official business. They used the same method twice more on the way out of the city—both times the surprised motorists seemed happy to lend Captain America a hand. The uniform was all the authorization they needed, and they'd even agreed to his request to keep it to themselves for a day or two.

They drove all night, stopping several times to steal parked cars to further throw off their pursuers. Steve felt a degree of guilt, but he didn't see what choice they had. By lunchtime the next day, he had managed to get some guns and money from one of the supply caches that were scattered across the country, so he consoled himself by leaving a bundle of notes in the mailbox of the house that they took the next car from. He had chosen a cache that he had personally created, knowing that S.H.I.E.L.D. would be monitoring the ones they knew about, searching for any sign of the fugitives. It had seemed paranoid at the time, but he had wanted to make sure that he had resources of his own, and that decision was now paying off.

Day bled into night, and the drive became a blur of rest stops, greasy food, and what seemed like gallons of coffee. They took turns driving, one at the wheel while the other two tried to sleep, but they were soon irritable and ready for the next step.

"So what happens now?" Katherine asked. "We can't keep driving like this forever."

"It already feels like forever," Karl muttered under his breath.

"I heard that," she snapped. "Can we be serious here for a moment?"

"It's a fair question," Steve said. "I'm not sure what to do. Every agency in the country, maybe in the world, will be after you. And there's still the bounty. There are only so many daring escapes we can make before our luck runs out."

"So what are the options?" she asked.

"I can try and get you fake documents, but we'll have to leave the country, lay low for a while."

"Cap, with all due respect, that's not going to work."

"Why?"

"You're one of the most recognizable men in the world. It won't matter where you go, someone would end recognizing you, and you'd be asked for your autograph."

"So what are you saying?" Steve asked, even though he had a pretty good idea where the other man was going.

"I think maybe it's time for us to say good-bye," Karl said. "Katherine and I go one way, you go another."

"I'm not going to just abandon you."

"You're not. Katherine and I can blend in anywhere. Do you know how many college girls go on an overseas holiday? As for me, Uncle Sam spent a whole lot of money on training me to look just like one of the locals anywhere I went. I wouldn't have survived an hour in some of the places they sent me if I couldn't. But you? You can't blend in—it's a simple as that," Karl said. "Look, I know you want to help us, but you just make getting caught inevitable."

Steve slammed his hand into the wheel, hard. He knew the other man was right, but he didn't like it.

"He's right, Steve," Katherine said gently. "You've done so much for me, and I'll never forget it, but you can't do any more for us."

"It's okay, Cap. This is something I'm very good at. We did this thing all the time at the Foundation. Katherine and I will go off the grid, and when we reappear, it will be with brand new identities. Katherine can take the time to decide what she wants to do with her research."

Katherine looked at Karl strangely. "We?"

"Yes, we. There is no way in the world that I'm going to let you go off on your own. I believe in this cause as much as you do."

"Is that so? The cause, huh?" Katherine said, an odd note in her voice. "Interesting."

Karl flushed. "That's right. I have all the contacts we need, and if Cap can give us some seed money, we'll be set."

"Where will you—never mind, maybe it's best that I don't know," Steve said. "Yes, it's definitely for the best."

"So, where do we say good-bye?" Katherine asked.

Steve looked at the road sign coming up in front of them, and smiled.

"I have an idea."

* * *

They stood in the middle of a massive granite disk, looking down at the brass plate at its center.

"This is a nice touch, Cap," Karl said.

Surrounding them was a large circle of darker stone divided into four segments by two crossing lines etched into the concrete. Each segment was labeled with a name of a state—Utah, Colorado, New Mexico, and Nevada.

"This place has always fascinated me. It's called a quadripoint, but it's more than just the four states that meet here—there are two federally recognized Native American nations here as well," Steve said. "It seems like fate that we're here, don't you think?"

The other two nodded.

"It feels full of possibilities, doesn't it?" Katherine asked. "You could go anywhere from here."

"I'm going to stay here awhile, and just . . . enjoy the setting. You two go, choose a direction, and disappear. I'll do the same, head off to a random state for a few days before I go home, try and lay some false trails, make sure that any eyes are on me while you two disappear. And, if I don't know where you are, no one can make me betray you."

Katherine wrapped her arms around Steve, squeezing him so hard that his still-bruised ribs twinged.

"Thank you, Steve—for everything. But, most of all, thank you for trusting me."

He looked down at her.

"I should be thanking you. You reminded me what it is I'm fighting for. Trusting you is easy—I know you'll make the right choice."

She stretched up on her tiptoes and kissed him softly on the corner of his mouth.

"Good-bye, Steve." She walked toward the parking lot, not looking back even once, leaving him alone with Karl.

"I promise I'll take good care of her, Cap," the ex-Marine said. "I'll die before I let anything happen to her."

"I know you will," Steve said. "I just wish I could come with you."

Karl winked. "Same old story, the Marines having to finish the job that the Army started."

"Karl, it's been an honor."

Karl snapped to attention and flashed Steve a salute.

"The honor has been mine, Captain."

Steve returned his salute.

"You take care, Marine."

Steve watched Karl walk away before turning back to the monument. He knelt and traced the brass plate with his fingers. He straightened and turned to read the inscription that encircled him.

"Here meet, in freedom, under God, four states."

Steve took that as a sign that freedom had been served today. He reached into his pocket and pulled out the first coin that he found. He stared at it for a moment, and then flicked it up into the air. It glittered in the sun, hanging at the zenith of its climb for a brief moment before plummeting back to the ground. The coin hit the concrete with a clink of metal and bounced a few times, rolling in ever-decreasing circles before toppling over and coming to a rest. Steve read the name of the state on the segment where the coin lay and smiled. It looked like he was going to Utah.

Epilogue

Steve sat at his desk, putting the last few touches on the scale model of a Flying Fortress bomber that he'd been given for his last birthday. He'd been working on it for days, and it was almost perfect, right down to the decals that he was filling in with a tiny paintbrush. In the background, the soft sound of Vera Lynn flowed from his radio, the familiar lyrics of "We'll Meet Again" bringing back bittersweet memories. He tried not to think about all the people he had had to say good-bye to over the years; some he had lost to the war, and some he had lost to the gulf of time. How many of his friends had died, or aged beyond recognition, while he had lain slumbering beneath the ice?

Those thoughts led to memories of his latest good-byes, and he wondered what Karl and Katherine were doing right now. He hoped they were lounging on a beach somewhere, drinking fruit-laden cocktails and making gentle fun of one another. That's what he would be doing, if he were them. But, knowing their passions, he wouldn't be surprised if they were doing volunteer work in a developing country instead, perhaps setting up internet access for some remote village. There was no shortage of places that they could be, but wherever they were, he simply hoped that they were happy—and safe.

Once they had gone their separate ways, Steve had rented a Ford Mustang and crisscrossed Utah, driving with the top down and the wind in his hair. After what he considered a suitable amount of time, he had driven back cross country. He'd made sure that he'd been seen at rest stops and gas stations, acting as if he were trying to keep a low profile, but making sure that enough people saw him that word would get back to the right ears. He'd actually enjoyed the time away checking out the state—the only issue had been the uncertainty, the not knowing where Karl and Katherine were going, and whether they were okay.

After he returned, he had been called in for an interview with S.H.I.E.L.D., where they demanded he justify his actions and that he reveal the location of Karl and Katherine. Once he had made it clear he didn't know their whereabouts, there wasn't much S.H.I.E.L.D. could do to him, especially given who he was. Sometimes, there was a lot to be said for his high profile. Pushing him too hard was not good for one's career, and that fact had earned him a lot of latitude. It wasn't something he liked making a habit of—that way led to corruption—but he thought that in this case, he had earned a break. An hour later he was out, and he doubted that he would be bothered again.

In the days following his release, various agencies tried to get information out of him, trying to piece together as much of Katherine's research as they could. As he genuinely didn't know anything about her work, it had been easy to get rid of them. He had taken a great deal of pleasure in watching various agents tear their hair out as they had tried to explain the basic concepts of coding to him and he had deliberately asked increasingly stupid questions.

There had been appeals to his patriotism, offers of money, threats of disciplinary action—every strategy they could think of to try to convince to lure Katherine out of hiding, but he had been immovable. There had been visits from increasingly senior figures, both military and civilian, but he had continued to present the same smiling obduracy. Politicians had been noticeable in their absence, however— it was if they could sense the approaching cloud of scandal and wanted no part of it. In the end, his threats to reveal the existence of Ex Umbra had scared enough people and prevented too much pressure being brought to bear.

Finally, he had just been issued a caution—to which he paid as much attention as he normally did to anything that he felt was bureaucratic rubbish—and was told he had two weeks of furlough, during which it was strongly recommended that he stay away from government buildings. He wasn't worried; he knew that as soon as there was another emergency that required his particular talents, he would be called upon, and that all would be forgiven. He hadn't been worried that there would be any other consequences of a more permanent nature—making Katherine or Karl disappear would have been simple enough, but if Captain America vanished, serious questions would be asked.

Now, he was just spending some time enjoying some well-earned rest and relaxation. He'd managed to get hold of all twenty-one of those mysteries he had enjoyed so much at the cabin, and he had several more models to work on. He'd also bought himself a computer tutorial book, something for dummies, and he planned to give his skills in that area a serious upgrade. He was actually quite happy to be forced to take time off, otherwise he had a tendency toward overwork. At least this way, he could do what he wanted without feeling guilty about it.

He found working on models deeply relaxing—something about the imposition of order on the chaotic arrangement of parts that came in the little plastic bag. Since he had gotten home, over the space of three days he had already assembled two. One had been an M4 Sherman tank; the other, the English fighter plane that had caused the Germans so many problems: the Spitfire.

Steve was self-aware enough to know why he always

chose models from a particular era—there was something soothing about being transported back to that time in his life. It might have been a time of constant danger, but he had always felt alive and that he was doing something worthwhile with his life. Most of all, it was a world that he understood—a world that he was part of. This new world had its good points, but he would always be a man out of time. It was nice to have something familiar to look at.

Once he finished the Boeing B-17 Flying Fortress, he wasn't sure what would be next. Maybe something a little more ambitious—an aircraft carrier or one of the more advanced weapons that Howard Stark and his colleagues had developed to combat the war machines that Hydra had seemed to churn out in a never-ending procession.

The ringing of the phone pulled him out of his thoughts. He frowned. There were very few people who had his phone number, and none that he was particularly interested in talking to right now. If it had been an emergency, the much more hi-tech transceiver currently sitting in his sock drawer would have called for his attention. He turned back to the model, deciding that the caller could leave a message if it was important, and that he would check once he had completed painting the roundel that he was working on.

The phone continued to ring insistently, nagging at him

to answer it. Twice he just caught himself before he made a mess of the fine detail he was working on, and finally he capitulated and picked it up.

"Steve Rogers speaking."

"Hello, Steve," a familiar voice said.

"Maria!" Steve said, genuine pleasure in his voice. "How are you?"

"Can't complain. And you?"

"Pretty good. I've just had a few very relaxing weeks interstate. Now I'm just puttering around the house. Catching up on a few projects."

"Sounds lovely. Wish I could say the same—it's been crazy here. I've been putting out fires left, right, and center."

"Sorry to hear that," Steve said. "Sounds pretty stressful."

"Sure is. Look, Steve, the reason I'm calling . . . have you turned on the television lately?"

"No, I don't like watching it when I'm working in the den. It's distracting, and to be completely honest, I find a lot of what's on these days either utterly incomprehensible or a bit stress inducing."

"I think maybe you should make an exception today, Steve. Can you do that—for me?"

"I guess so . . ."

Steve reached into a drawer and pulled out a remote. He pointed it at the wall above the radio and pressed a button.

A panel slid across, revealing a large plasma flat-screen. He pressed another button, and it lit up.

"Any particular channel?"

"Any news channel will do. Maybe even some of the non-news channels. This is big enough."

Steve flicked it over until he found a news feed.

. . . New computer virus "Ex Umbra" cripples China censorship tech . . .

. . . Riots in Eastern Africa as freedom protests topple government . . .

. . . Mass resignations in both United States political parties as new scandals come to light . . .

The screen filled with story after story of political chaos rippling across the world, of oppressive regimes shaken to their foundations as information-starved populaces consumed their fill from an unfettered internet.

He picked up the phone again.

"Interesting times."

"Yes, they are. Lots of governments are very scared right now—seems this new virus is playing havoc with internet filters and firewalls. Lots of people are suddenly seeing the world with fresh eyes, and realizing there's more to life than what their government has been telling them. I think we're going to see a lot of changes in a lot of places."

"What about our government, are they scared?" Steve asked.

"Why would they be? They've got nothing to hide, right?" Maria asked.

"That's good to know."

A clear chime echoed down the line.

"What was that?" Steve asked. "Are we being listened in on?"

"Just the opposite, in fact. That was telling us that this line is secure. My scan just finished," Maria said. "So, Steve, is this what you hoped for?"

"I don't know what I hoped for. All I know is, I think that we're going to see some changes in a world that desperately needs them."

"Always the optimist, aren't you, Steve? So, you think we did the right thing?"

"I think so," Steve said. "But, how are you, really? I heard you made a bad decision at work."

"Steve, I told you—the line is secure. Stop trying to be subtle—it doesn't suit you," she said. "As far as everyone is concerned, I did everything I could to make sure the research ended up back in our government's hands, including arresting a member of my family and Captain America himself. No one suspects that I had anything to do with you getting away, and my superiors bought my story about you jumping me. The video—and the bruises—looked very convincing, and it would be pretty unreasonable for anyone to blame me for coming out second best to you. In the end, there wasn't even an reprimand put on my record."

"You really did have it all worked out," Steve said admiringly. "But, if they had suspected?"

"They would have needed more than suspicion before they moved on me," Maria said. "There are plenty of secrets left in this world, despite this computer virus, and I know more than a few that people wouldn't want unearthed. I'm pretty safe."

"That's good to hear," Steve said. "I'd hate to have to get used to someone new around S.H.I.E.L.D. At my age, change is tough."

He was pleased when she laughed at that one. Maybe they were making progress.

"I have to say, Steve, I do like the name that they gave it. Jonah must be furious. Next time I visit the prison he's in, I might go make sure he knows about it."

"I guess it's something for him to cling to, that the name will live on even though the agency has been shut down," Steve said. "It has been shut down, right?"

Maria hesitated.

"I hope it has," she said. "Some of its assets have been absorbed by other agencies, and the operatives who could be demonstrated to have violated the law have been prosecuted—Jonah among them. But he still isn't talking, no matter what threat or incentive we offer. He won't give up any names—not who he answered to, or the agents he might have left."

"He was a true believer, I'll give him that," Steve said grudgingly. It was hard to give Jonah any credit—Steve still had very vivid memories of the session with the Tasers. "He honestly believed that he was part of something noble, and that sort of man would rather be a martyr than betray his faith."

"Well, at least know we know about the threat, and we can watch for it," Maria said. "We are currently doing a top-to-bottom shakedown, checking every member of S.H.I.E.L.D., and I have it on good authority pretty much every other government agency is doing the same."

"I'm glad to hear it," Steve said. "And General Ross?"

"Secretary Ross, you mean," Maria corrected him. "He was just assisting an existing government resource in their normal operations, nothing more—according to him anyway. He didn't create Ex Umbra, and is taking none of the blame for their actions, and he's claiming complete ignorance of their extralegal activities."

"Very convenient," Steve said, resolving that he would be wary of Ross in the future. "So, who did know?"

"No one, or at least no one willing to say so, anyway," Maria said. "We aren't going to let this go, though. Someone will answer for it—eventually."

Steve grunted skeptically. "We'll see."

"I do have some more bad news for you," Maria said.

"Go on."

"Your other friend, the caped intruder. He escaped."

"What!" Steve yelled. "How?"

"The Ex Umbra facility was complete chaos, and by the time we had established some sort of order, he was gone," she said. "Somehow, in the confusion, he managed to just walk out of there."

"I guess I had better keep an eye out for him. His professional pride will demand a rematch," Steve said. "I'll try to think of some new tricks to show him. At least I know that I'll be his priority. He'll come for me at his first opportunity, rather than for . . . someone else. Besides, I doubt he will have any more luck finding a certain someone than any of the dozen agencies currently searching have."

"Well, about that, Steve." Maria paused on the other end of the line. "It leads into my other reason for calling you. There's a question I have for you."

"Shoot," he said warily.

"Steve, have you heard from them? They've dropped completely off the radar, in fact, if it weren't for this virus, I would be worried they were dead in a ditch somewhere. It's very impressive, actually."

Steve smiled. He'd guessed Karl hadn't been exaggerating about his talent and experience in that area.

"Sorry, Maria, not a word. I didn't really expect anything, though, that was part of the plan."

"Not a word?"

"I swear to you, not a single word," Steve said solemnly.

There was silence on the other end.

"Maria?"

"Steve, would you tell me if you knew where they were?"

He didn't even hesitate.

"No."

"No?" A degree of frost crept into her voice. "You don't think that you can trust me?"

"What, you don't think between the bug and the lies, you've given me good reason not to trust you?"

There was another silence at the end of the line.

"Steve, I did what I had to do," she said. "It wasn't anything personal."

"I know, Maria. And strange as it may sound, I do trust you. But you've got your orders, and the fewer people who know a secret, the better. I don't even want to know, just in case I give it away."

"Fair enough." She sounded slightly mollified. "It would just be nice to know that they are okay, and happy."

"Yeah, I agree. Look, if I find out anything and I think it's safe, I'll let you know, okay?"

"Okay. I probably should get going and leave you to your

baseball cards, or whatever it is that you do with your spare time."

"Always a pleasure, Maria."

Steve hung up the phone and turned back to the television, watching the breaking news for a few minutes and smiling with satisfaction at each new story. Eventually, he grew bored and switched off the television, throwing the remote back into the drawer. He picked up his brush and dabbed at the model, his brush strokes surprisingly delicate for such a big man. The record finished, and there was only the soft hiss of the needle. Steve walked over to the radio and ran his hand along the polished wood. He flicked through the records, then stopped as if remembering something he should have done.

He opened the drawer that the remote had come from and pulled out a postcard. The back was completely blank, free of any message—not a single word. The front had a picture of a sandy white beach that glistened under the sun and drank up the turquoise waves that lapped against the shore. He stared at the postcard for a moment, a smile on his face, and then pinned it up on the corkboard above his desk.

"Have fun, kids," he murmured. "You've earned it."

Acknowledgments

Thank you to my editor, Michael Melgaard—it was an adventure, but we made it! And, as always, thank you to everyone at Joe Books for all of their help, and for this incredible opportunity.

Most of all, a big thank you must go to my long-suffering wife for her patience with this one; I know I wasn't much fun to live with—when I was even around! I couldn't have done it without her love and support.

This book was written with the help of Scrivener and Dropbox, two of the best friends a writer can have.